Zaner-Bloser
HANDWRITING
A Way to Self-Expression

Grade K

Senior Authors

Clinton S. Hackney, Ed.D.
Language Arts Consultant

Virginia H. Lucas, Ph.D.
Professor of Education
Wittenberg University

Contributing Author:

Phoebe Ingraham, B.S.
Kindergarten Teacher
Milford (Ohio) Exempted Village Schools

Consultants:

Karen M. Csigas, Hammond (Ind.) City School District
E. Sue Godwin, Cumberland County (N.C.) School District
Eileen Rock, Camden (N.J.) City Schools
Susan K. Wilhelm, Sarasota County (Fla.) School District

Credits

Literature: "My Bicycle," "All of Me," "In the Apple Tree," "Five Baby Birds," "Eight Pigs," and "I Can Count" from *Finger Frolics*. Copyright © 1976, 1983 by Partner Press. Used by permission of the publisher. "The Yak" from *Zoo Doings* by Jack Prelutsky. Copyright © 1983 by Jack Prelutsky. Reprinted by permission of Greenwillow Books, a division of William Morrow & Co. "My Zipper Suit" by M. L. Allen (1935) from *Sung Under the Silver Umbrella*, sel. by the Literature Committee of the Association for Childhood Education International (p.33). New York: The MacMillan Company (27th printing, 1962). Reprinted by permission of M. L. Allen and the Association for Childhood Education International, 11141 Georgia Avenue, Ste. 200, Wheaton, MD. Copyright © 1962 by the Association. "The Little Turtle" by Vachel Lindsay from *Golden Whales*. Copyright © 1920 by Macmillan Publishing Company, renewed 1948 by Elizabeth C. Lindsay. Reprinted with permission of Macmillan Publishing Company. "P" (Let's have a picnic in the park) and "K" (A kettle's for the kitchen) from *Certainly, Carrie, Cut the Cake, Poems A to Z*. Copyright © 1971 by Margaret and John Travers Moore. Published by Bobbs-Merrill Co. Used by permission. "To Walk in Warm Rain" from *Speak Up* by David McCord. Copyright © 1979, 1980 by David McCord. By permission of Little, Brown and Company. "Snowman" from *One at a Time* by David McCord. Copyright © 1961, 1962 by David McCord. By permission of Little, Brown and Company. "Birthday Candles" from *Talking Time*, Second Edition, by Louise Binder Scott and J. J. Thompson. Copyright © 1966 by Louise Binder Scott and J. J. Thompson. Used by permission. "Umbrellas" from *Swing Around the Sun* by Barbara Juster Esbensen. Copyright © 1965 by Lerner Publications Company, 241 First Avenue North, Minneapolis, MN 55401. Reprinted by permission of the publisher. "Meg's Egg" from *Yellow Butter Purple Jelly Red Jam Black Bread* by Mary Ann Hoberman. Copyright © 1981 by Mary Ann Hoberman. Reprinted by permission of Gina Maccoby Literary Agency. "Quack! Quack!" from *Oh Say Can You Say?* by Dr. Seuss. Copyright © 1979 by Dr. Seuss and A. S. Geisel. "Just Three" from *All on a Summer Day* by William Wise. Copyright © 1971. Reprinted by permission of William Wise. "The Wish" by Ann Friday. Taken from *Read-Aloud Rhymes for the Very Young*, published by Alfred A. Knopf, Copyright © 1986. "The Vulture" by Hillaire Belloc. Taken from *The Random House Book of Poetry for Children* published by Random House, Inc. Copyright © 1983. "Nicholas Ned" by Laura E Richards, from *Sing a Song of Popcorn*. Copyright © 1988, Scholastic, Inc.

Art: Joe Boddy: pp. 3-25, 103-108; Kate Sturmar Gorman: pp. 26, 28, 30, 32, 34, 36, 38, 40, 42, 44, 46, 48, 50, 52, 54, 56, 58, 60, 62, 64, 66, 68, 70, 72, 74, 76, 78, 82; Dale Herron: pp. 84, 86, 88, 90, 92, 94, 96, 98, 100, 102.

Cover Photo: Aaron Haupt

ISBN 0-88085-160-0

Copyright © 1993 Zaner-Bloser, Inc.

All rights reserved. No part of this book may be reproduced or transmitted in any form or by any means, electronic or mechanical, including photocopying, recording, or by an information storage and retrieval system, without permission in writing from the Publisher. The Publisher has made every effort to trace the ownership of all copyrighted material and to secure the necessary permissions to reprint these selections. In the event of any question arising as to the use of any material, the Publisher, while expressing regret for any inadvertent error, will be happy to make any necessary corrections.
Zaner-Bloser, Inc., P. O. Box 16764, Columbus, Ohio 43216-6764
Printed in the United States of America

HOSPITAL
FIRE DEPARTMENT
LIBRARY
EMERGENCY
AMBULANCE
SCHOOL
SCHOOL BUS
TAXI
PARK

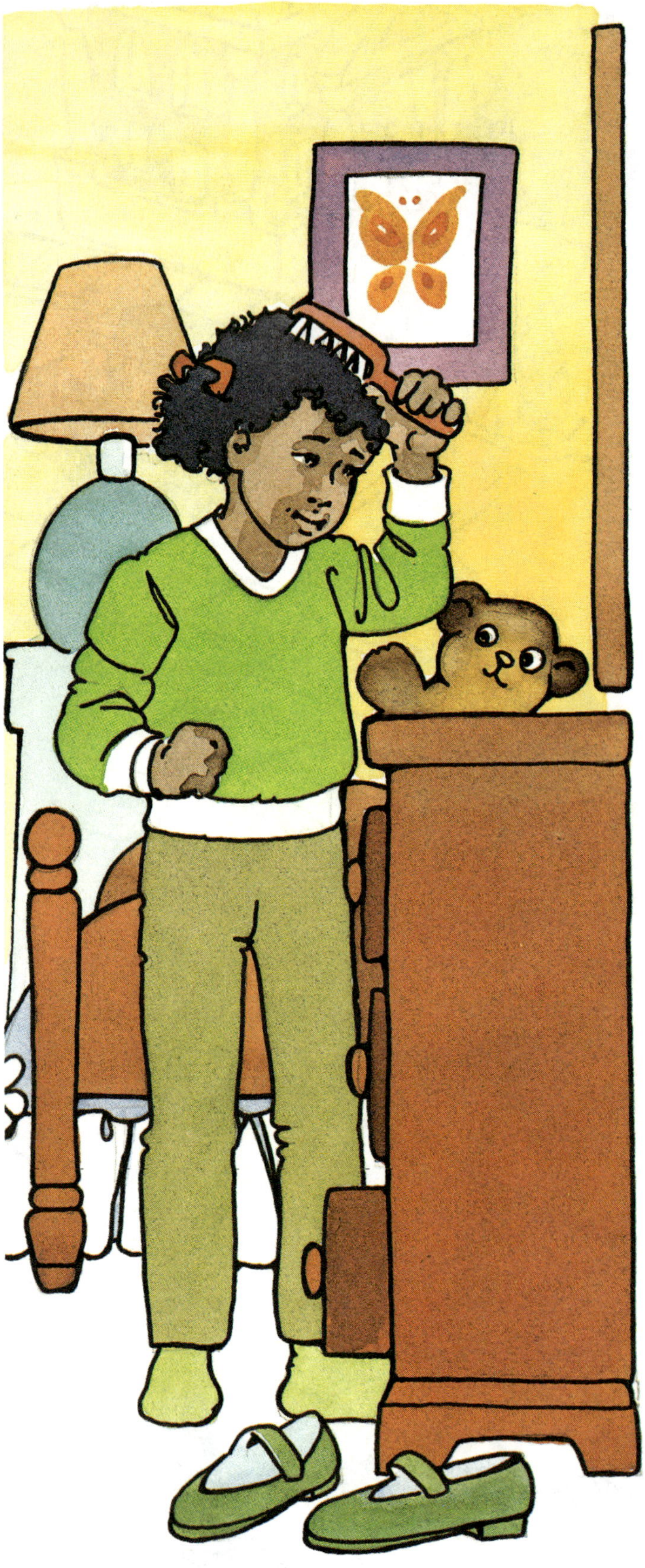

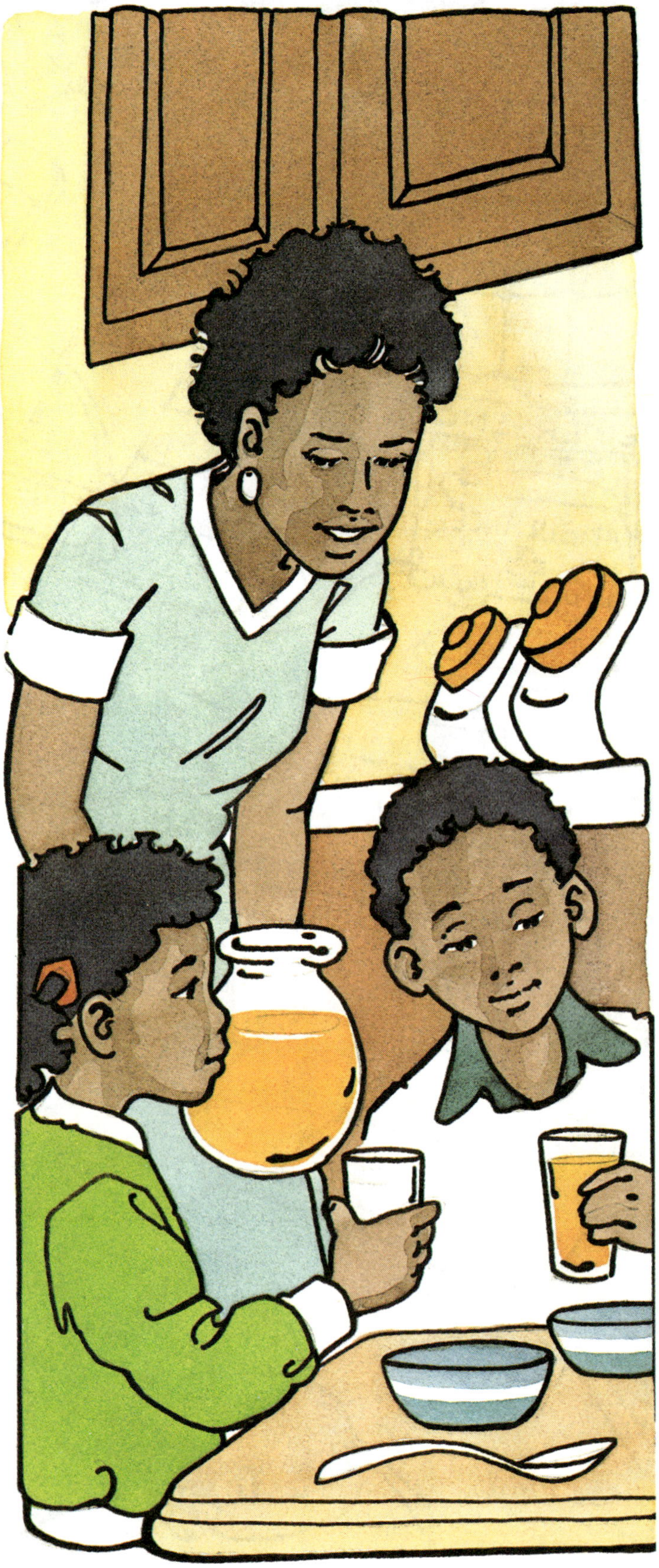

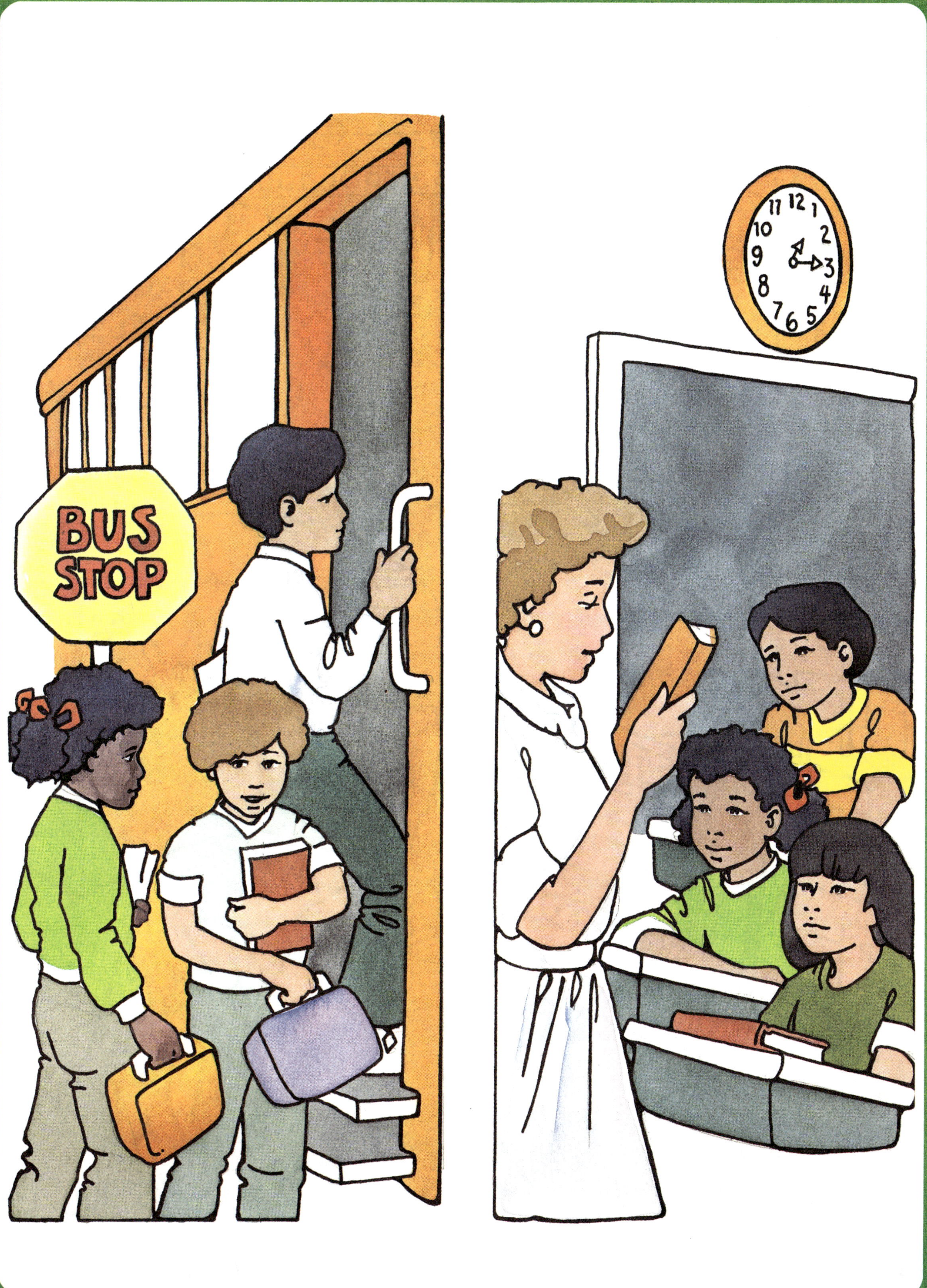
BUS
STOP

EXIT
SCHOOL BUS
OPEN
MOVE
MAIN
DON'T WALK
WALK
TOYS
PIZZA
KEEP OFF GRASS
SCHOOL CROSSING

MEAT
POULTRY
FISH
EMPLOYEES ONLY
VEGETABLES
MILK
AISLE TWO
SALE
AISLE ONE
FROZEN FOODS
FRUIT
DAIRY
DRINKS
COLD
BREAD

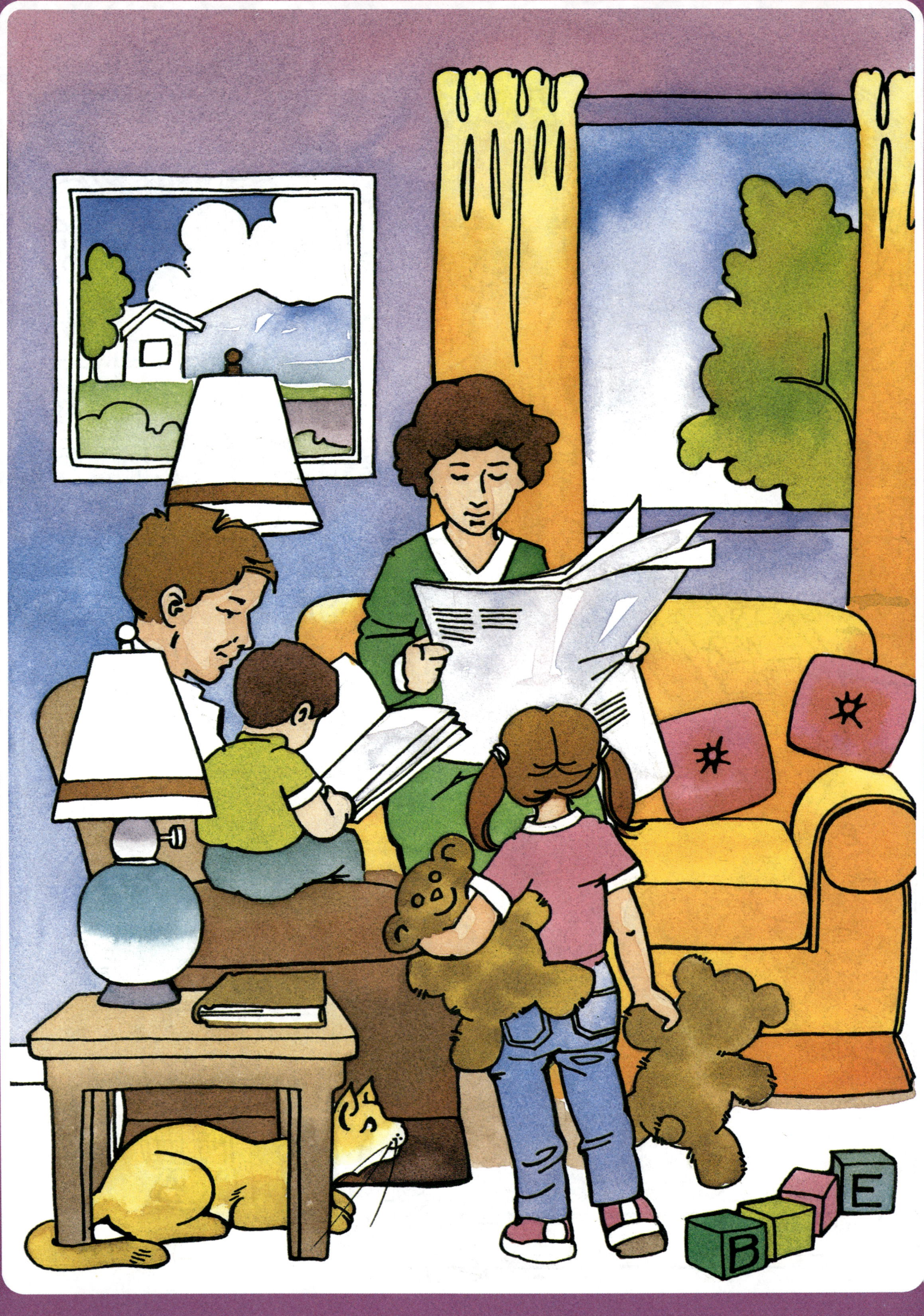
B
E

t   e   k

Match the objects.

Match the objects.

Match the shapes.

Color the shapes.

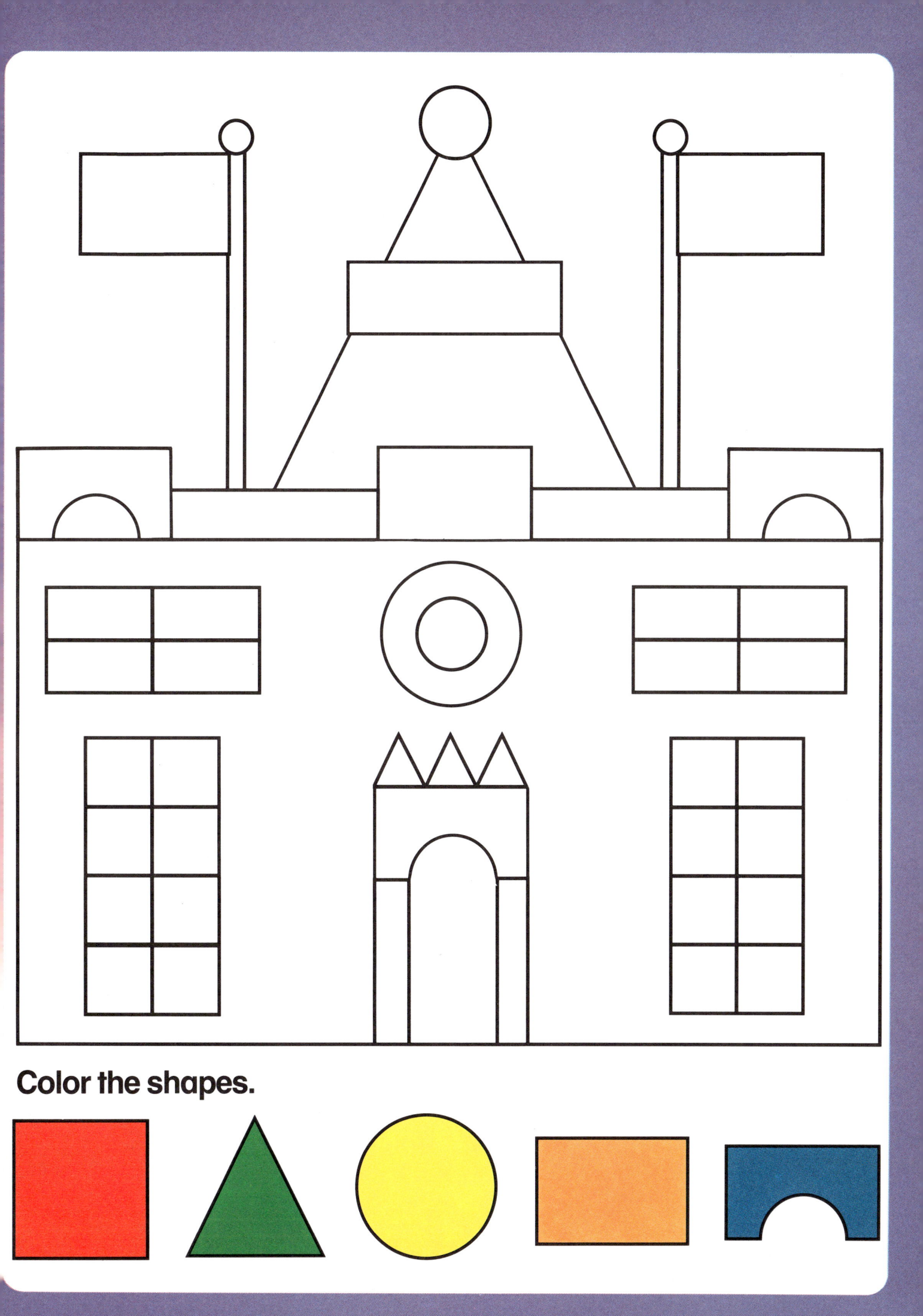

Match the letters.

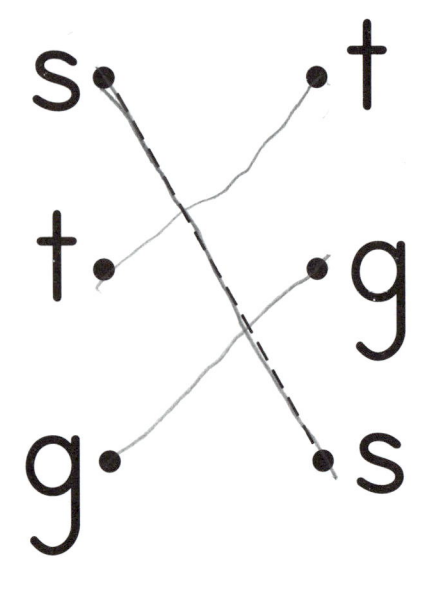

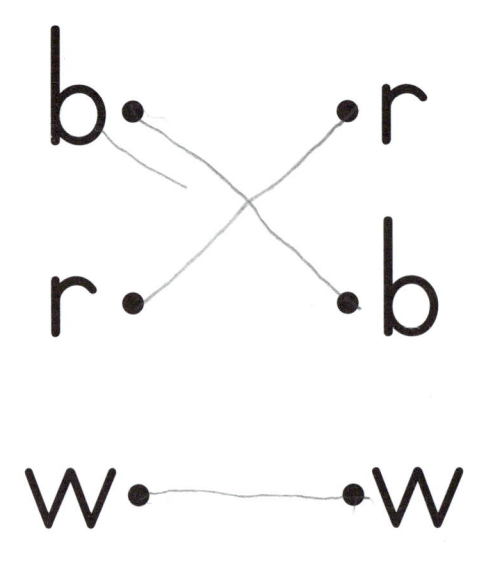

s • • t   b • • r

t • • g   r • • b

g • • s   w • — • w

[r] cry   [s] sun

[p] stop   [f] roof

14
Copyright © Zaner-Bloser, Inc.

Match the letters.

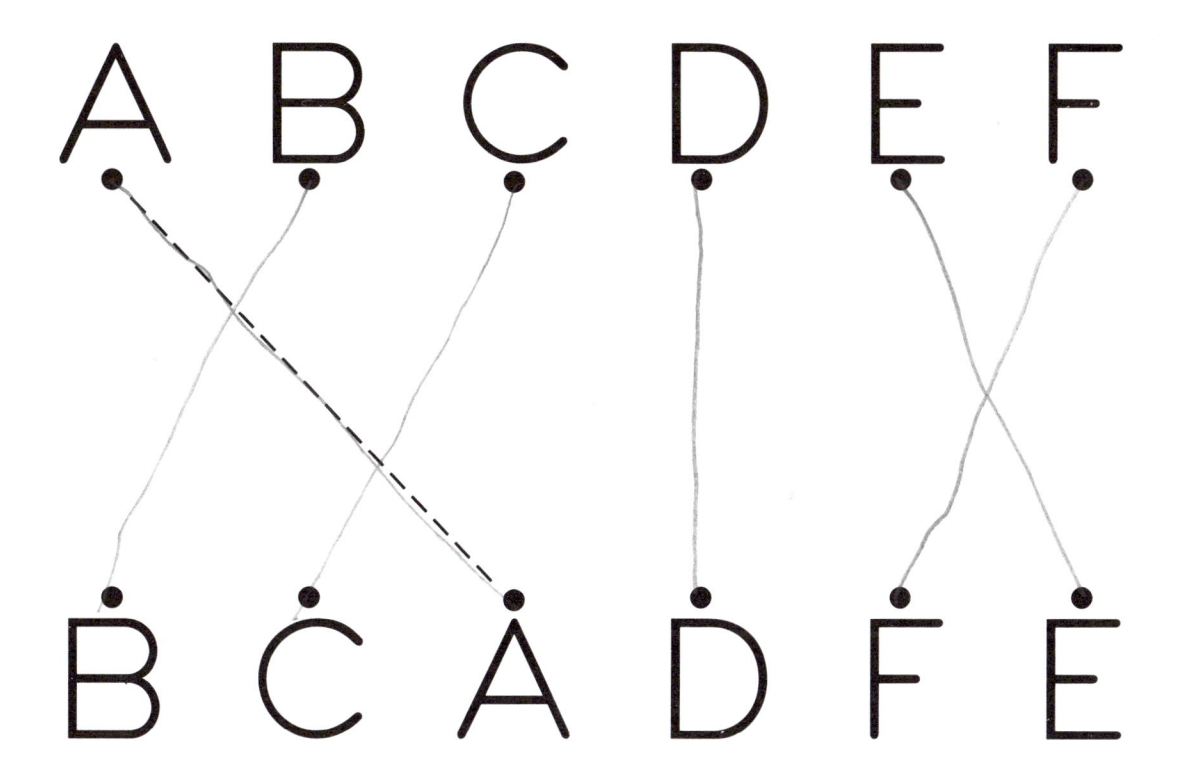

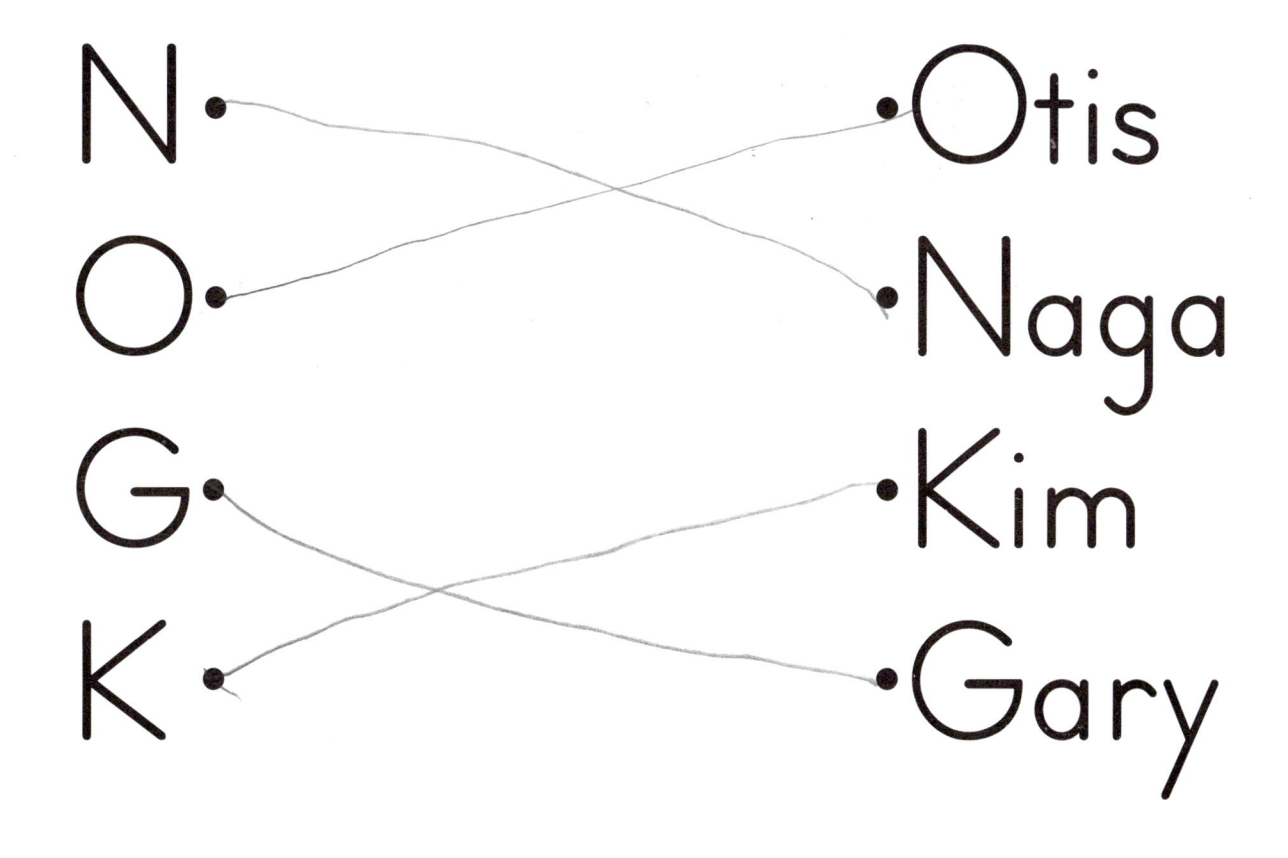

A B C D E F

B C A D F E

N O G K

Otis Naga Kim Gary

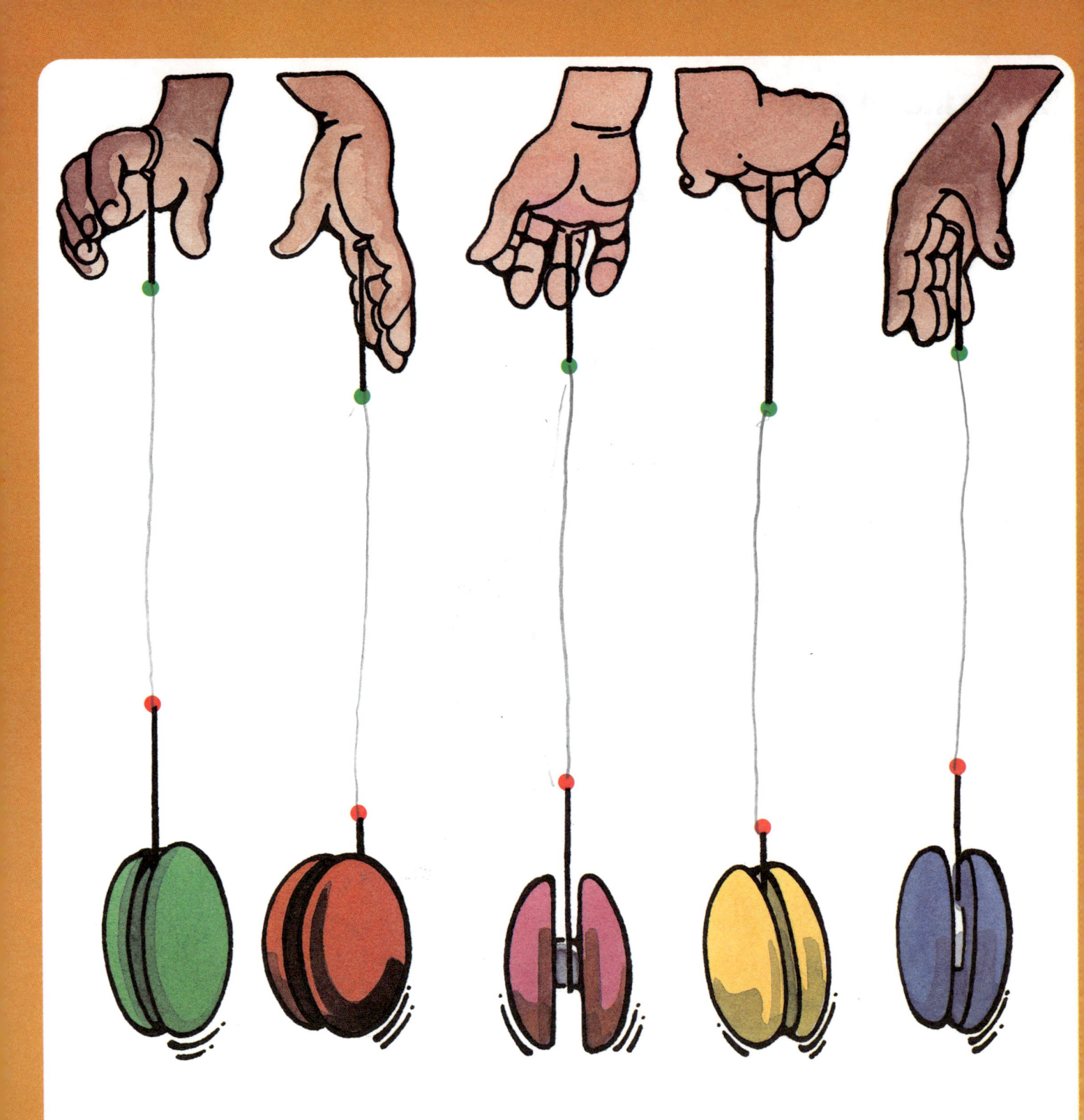

Trace and write.

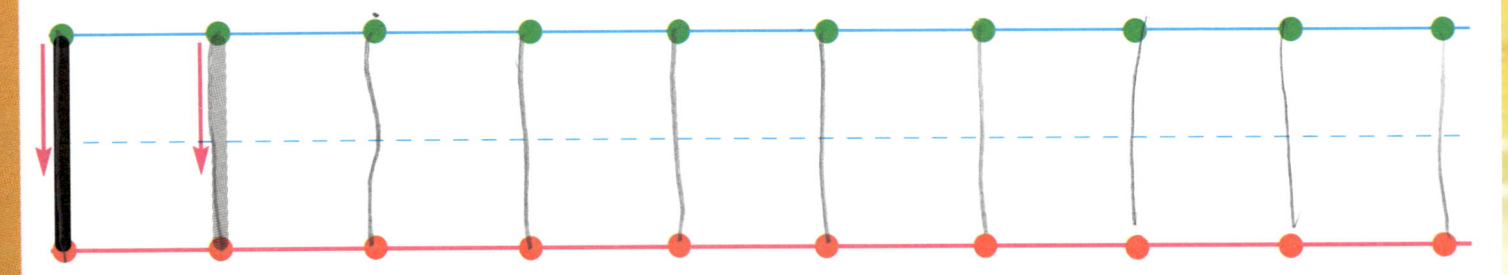

Trace and write.

Trace and write.

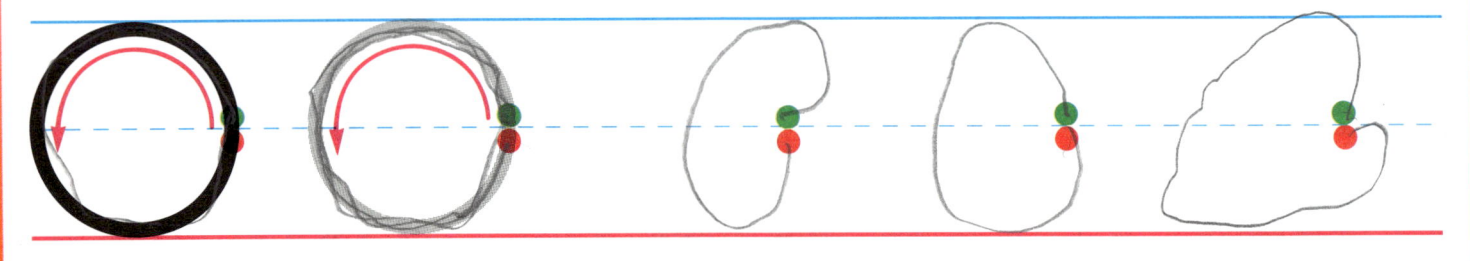

Trace and write.

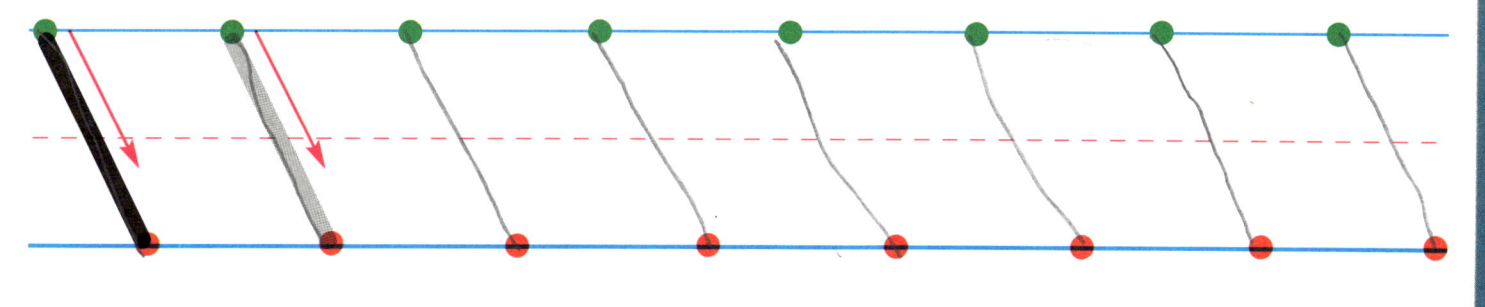

Trace and write.

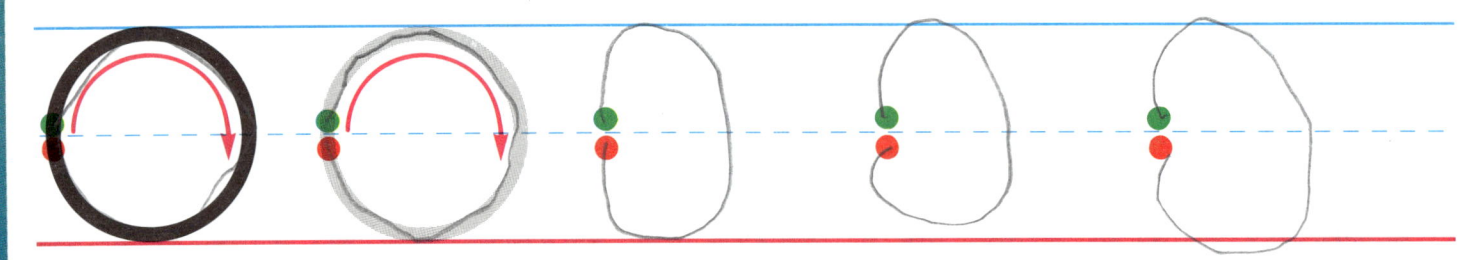

20

Trace and write.

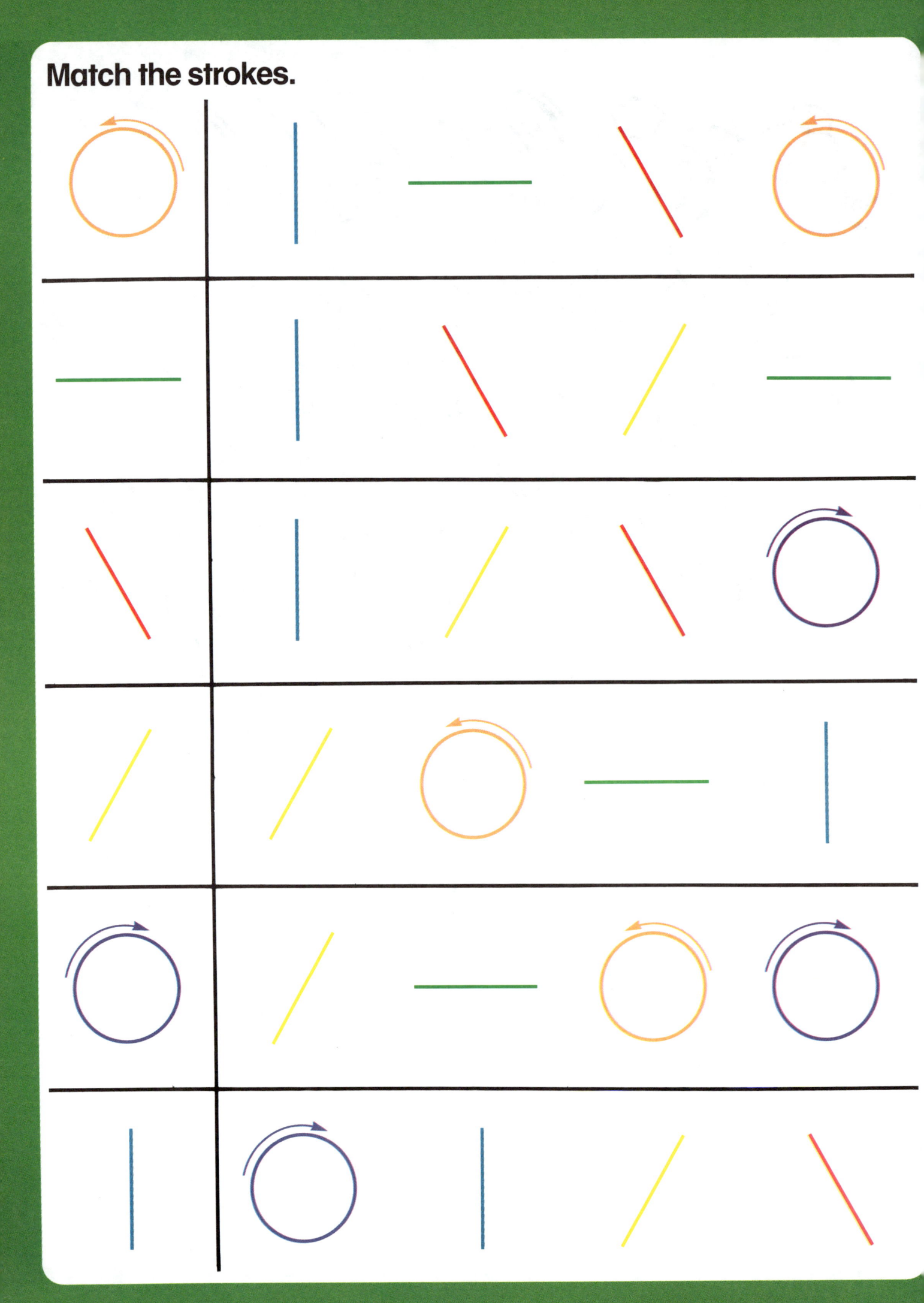

Match the strokes.

Match the strokes.

Draw the birdhouse.

Draw the snowman.

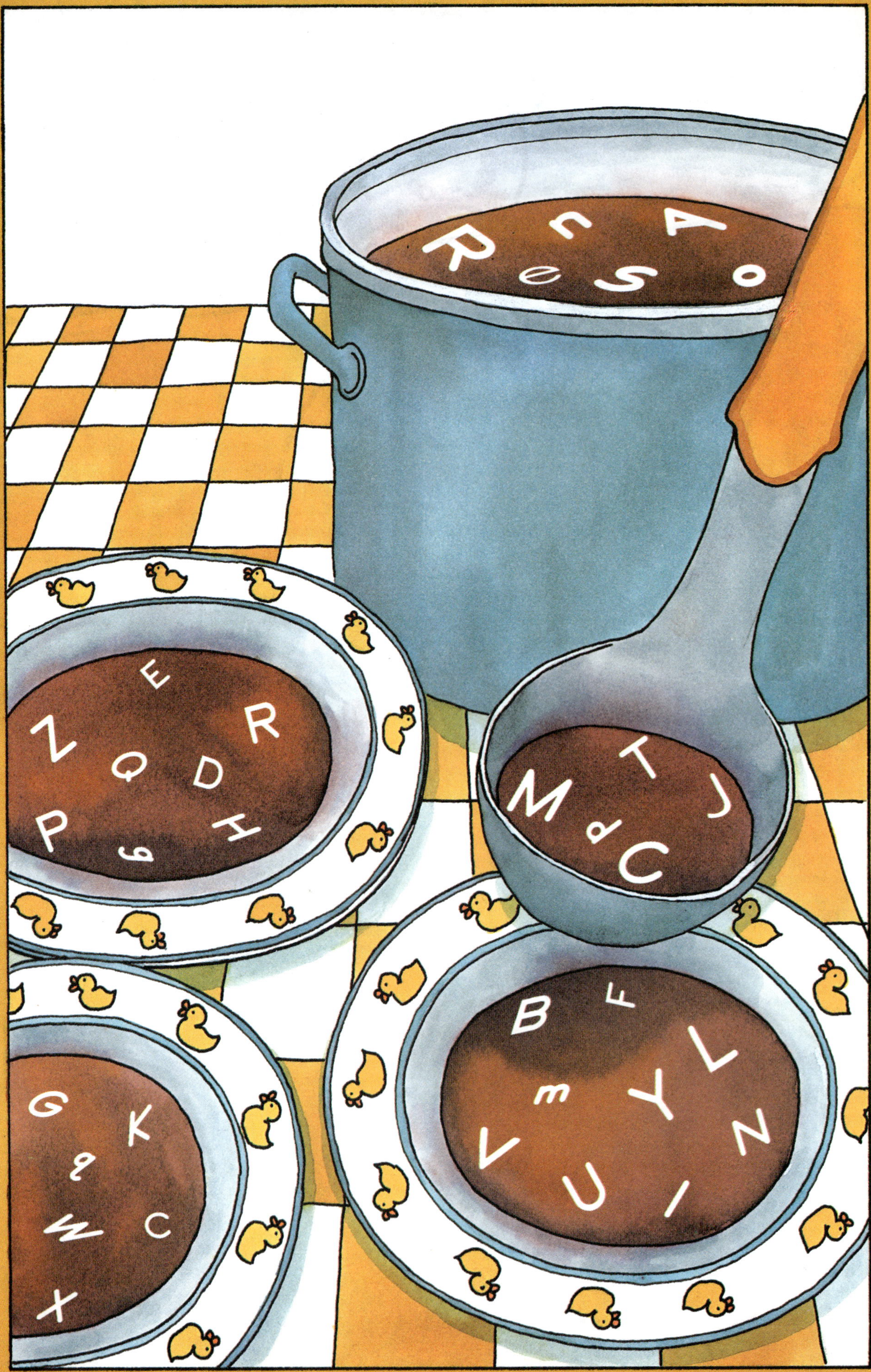

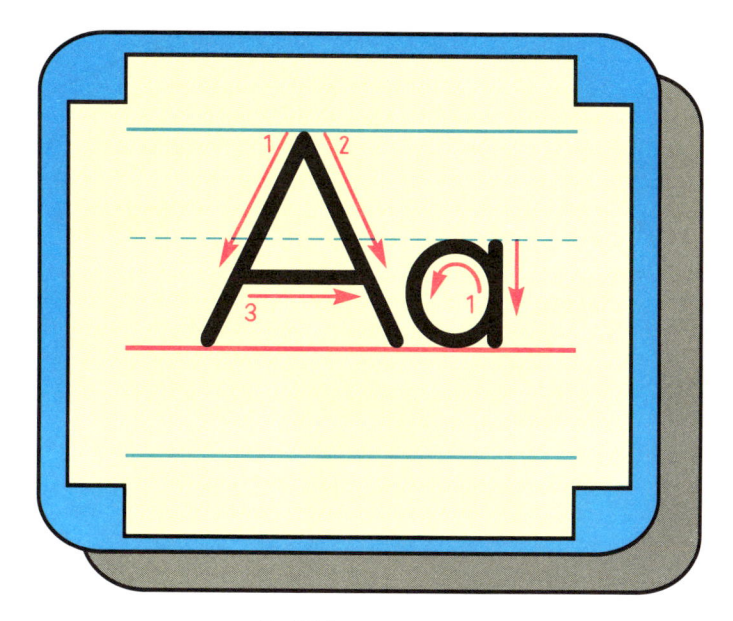

Alligator

Here is the alligator,
Sitting on a log.
Down in the pool,
He sees a little frog.

In goes the alligator,
Round goes the log,
Splash goes the water,
Away swims the frog!

Unknown

A a

Caterpillar

Caterpillar, caterpillar
Brown and furry,
Winter has come
And you better hurry.
Find a big leaf
Under which to creep.
Spin a cocoon
In which to sleep.
Then when warm weather
Comes this way
You'll be a butterfly
    and fly away.

                    Unknown

C c

32

Hey Diddle Diddle

Hey diddle diddle,
The cat and the fiddle,
The cow jumped over the moon.
The little dog laughed
To see such sport,
And the dish ran away with the spoon.

Mother Goose

D d

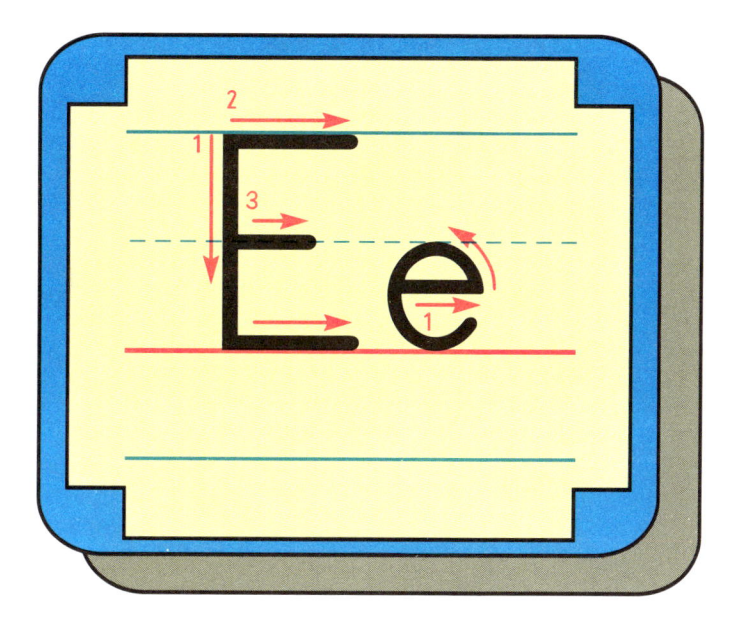

Meg's Egg

Meg
Likes
A *reg*ular egg
Not a poached
Or a fried
But a *reg*ular egg
Not a deviled
Or coddled
Or scrambled
Or boiled
But an *egg*ular
*Meg*ular
*Reg*ular
Egg!

Mary Ann Hoberman

E e

Fee, Fie, Fo, Fum

Fee, fie, fo, fum,
See my finger,
See my thumb.
Fee, fie, fo, fum,
Fingers gone,
So is thumb.

Unknown

F f

Safety

Red says STOP
And Green says GO.
Yellow says WAIT;
You'd better go slow!

When I reach a crossing place,
To left and right I turn my face.
I walk, not run, across the street,
And use my head to guide my feet.

                    Unknown

G g

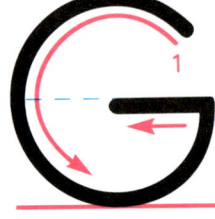

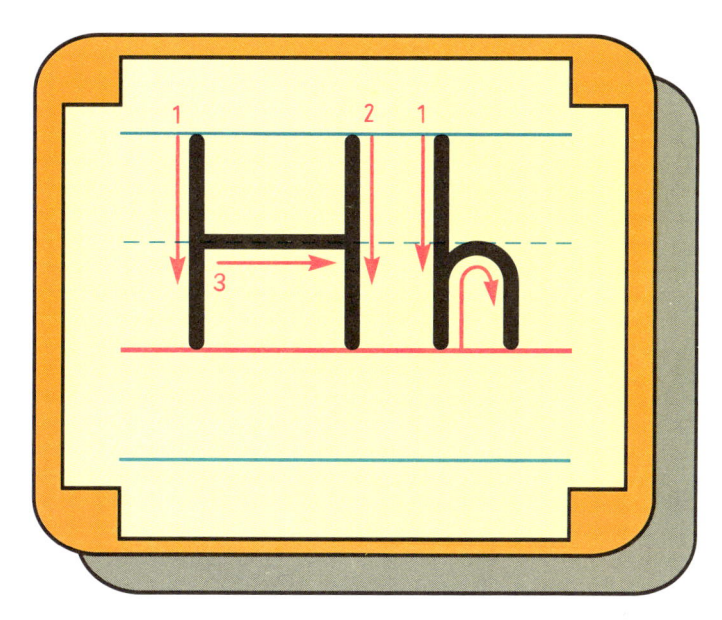

Humpty Dumpty

Humpty Dumpty sat on a wall,
Humpty Dumpty had a great fall;
All the King's horses, and all the King's men
Cannot put Humpty Dumpty together again.

Unknown

H h

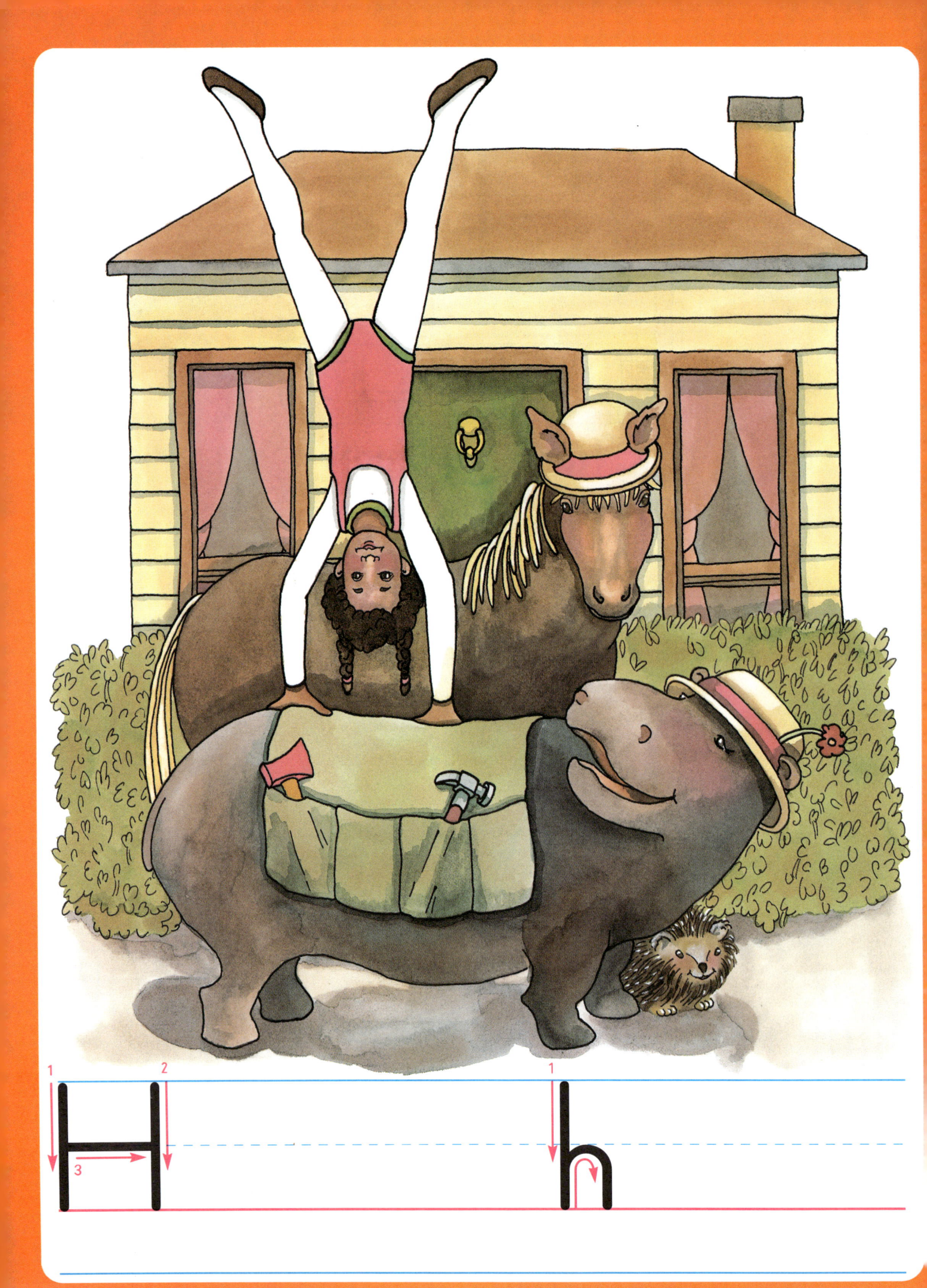

42

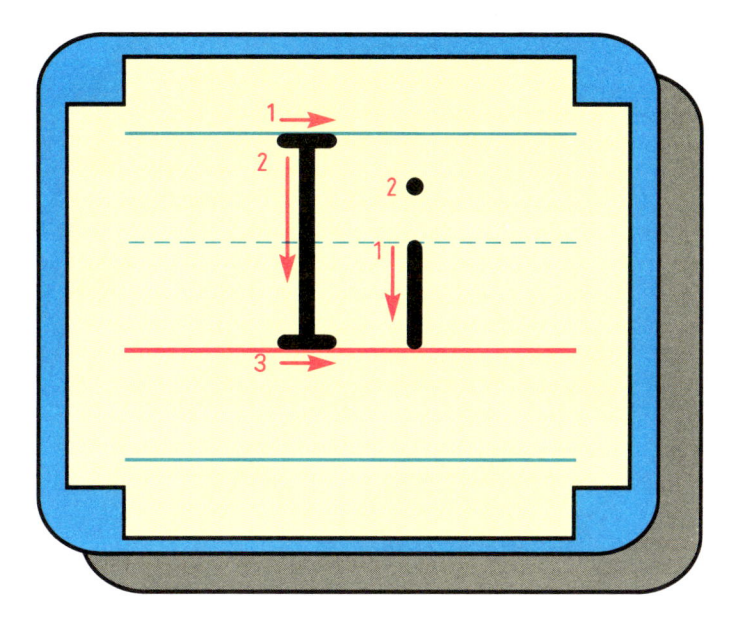

Icicles

We are little icicles,
Crying in the sun.
Can't you see our tiny tears
Dropping one by one?
                  Geraldine Lewis, age 12

Please Come!

I i

44

Jack Be Nimble

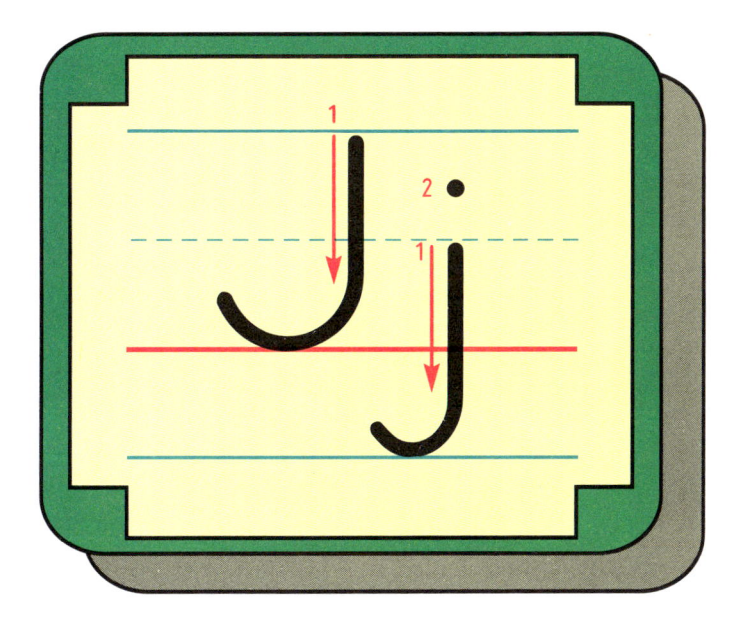

Jack be nimble,
Jack be quick,
Jack jump over
The candlestick.

Mother Goose

Jam   Jelly   Jelly

J   j

46

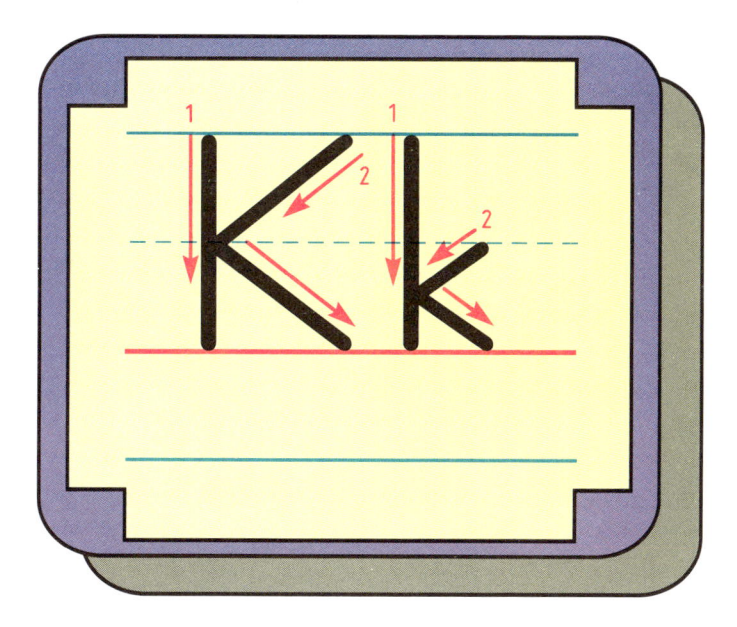

Kettle's for the Kitchen

A
Kettle's for the kitchen,
A key is for the door,
A kitten is for playing with
And keeping on the floor.

A kite is made for flying
When March winds blow,
Kindness is for everyone—
Didn't you know?

Margaret and John Travers Moore

K k

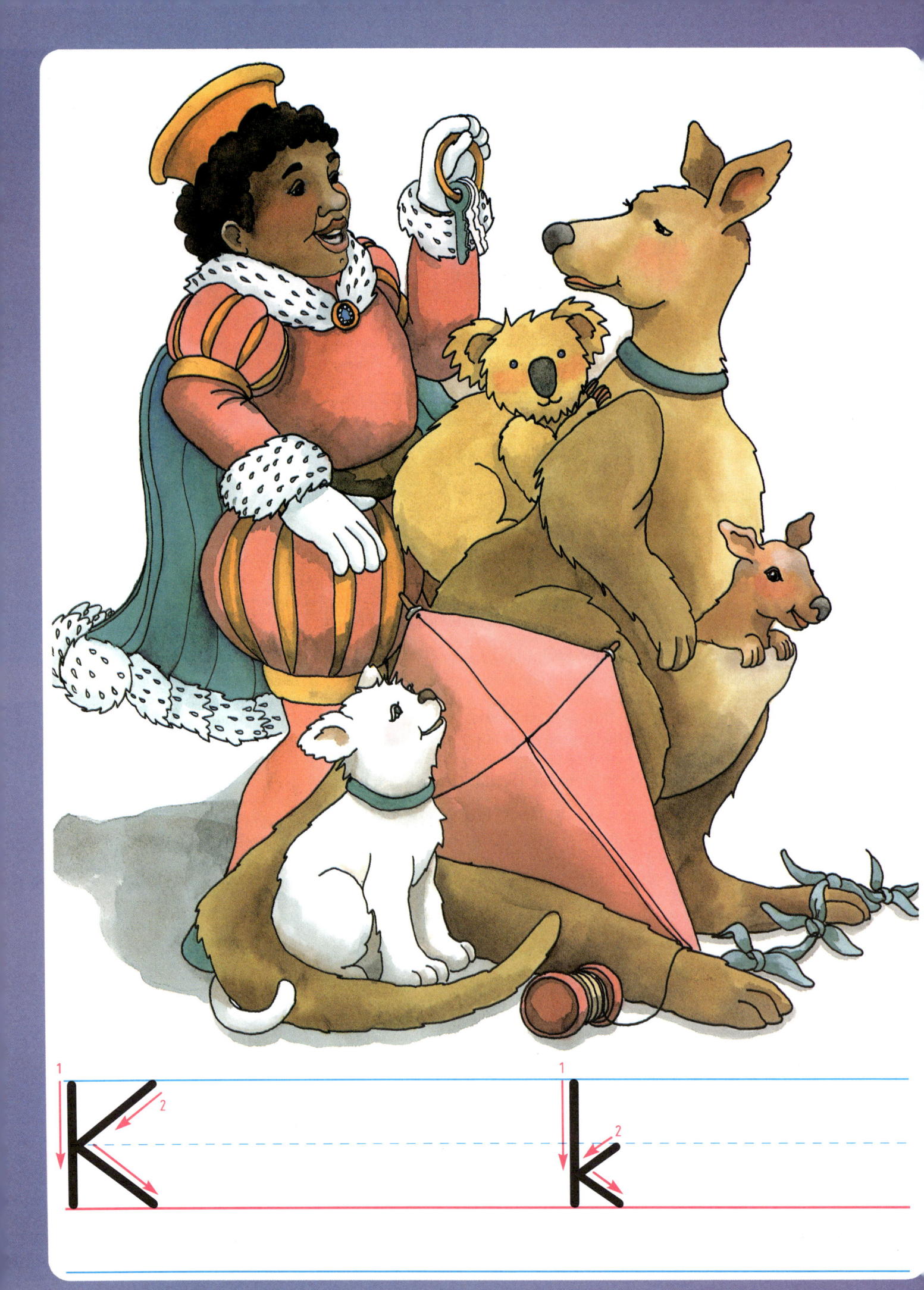

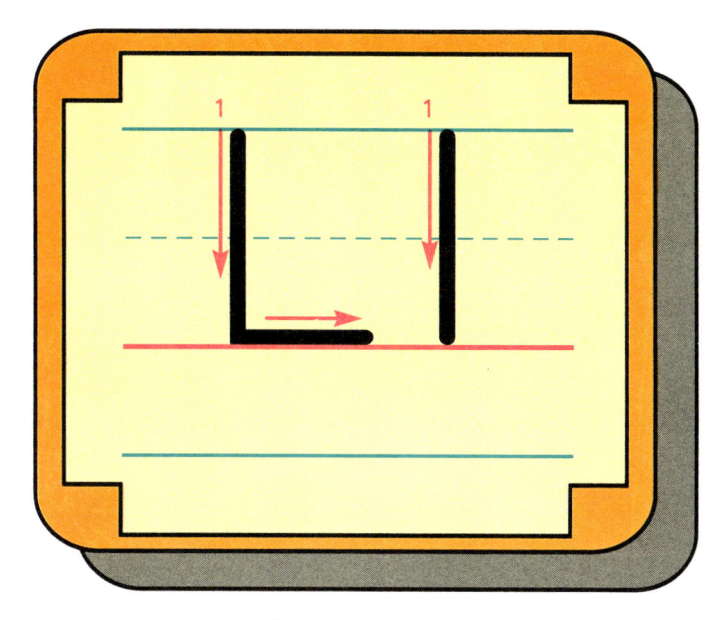

Leaves

Little leaves fall gently down,
Red and yellow, orange and brown.
Whirling, whirling round and round,
Quietly without a sound,
Falling softly to the ground.

Unknown

L l

50

My Maid Mary

My maid Mary she minds the dairy,
While I do a-hoeing and mowing each morn;
Gaily run the reel and the little spinning wheel.
While I am singing and mowing my corn.

Mother Goose

M m

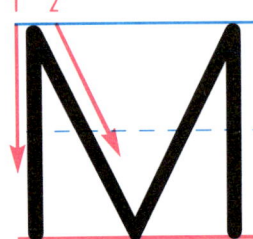

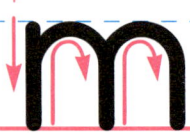

52

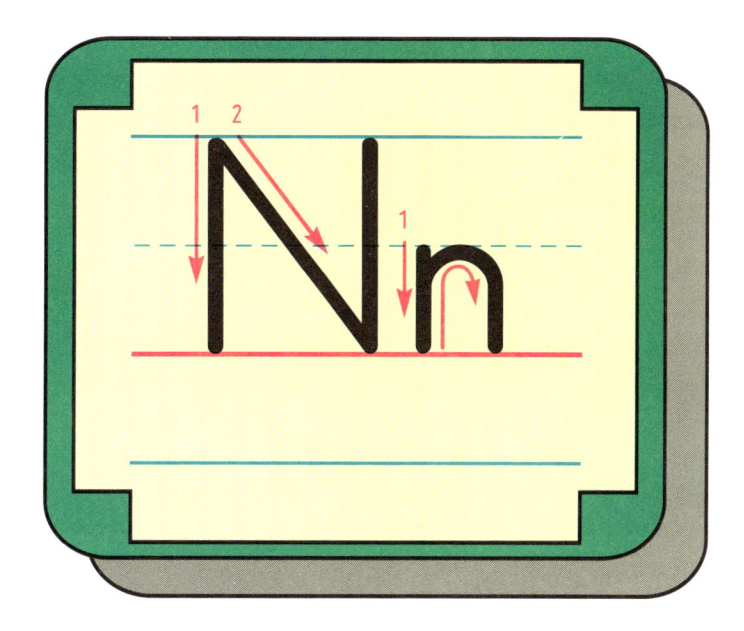

Nicholas Ned

Nicholas Ned,
He lost his head,
And put a turnip on instead;
But then, ah, me!
He could not see,
So he thought it was night, and he went to bed.

Laura E. Richards

N n

The Little Bird

Once I saw a little bird
    Come hop, hop, hop;
So I cried, "Little bird,
    Won't you stop, stop, stop?"
And was going to the window
    To say, "How do you do?"
But he shook his little tail,
    And far away he flew.

                      Mother Goose

56

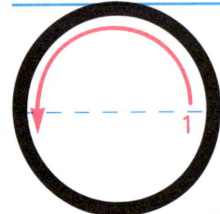

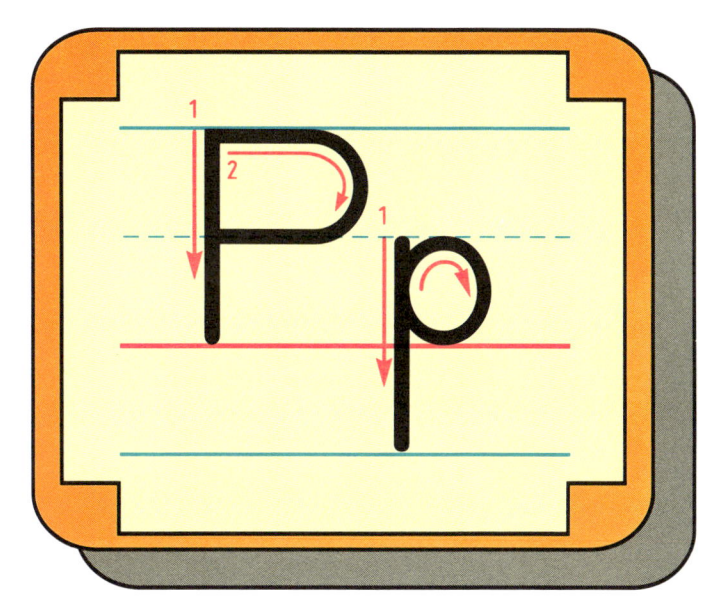

Let's Have a Picnic in the Park

Let's have a
Picnic in the park:
Pack a few pickles,
Peanut butter,
Plates,
Pepper and salt,
Potato salad,
Pie,
Pears and peaches,
Pop;
Add bread and meat
and you have plenty to eat—
To eat
Until
You stop.

Margaret and John Travers Moore

P p

58

Quack, Quack!

We have two ducks. One blue. One black.
And when our blue duck goes "Quack-quack"
our black duck quickly quack-quacks back.
The quacks Blue quacks make her quite a quacker
but Black is a quicker quacker-backer.

                      Dr. Seuss

Q q

60

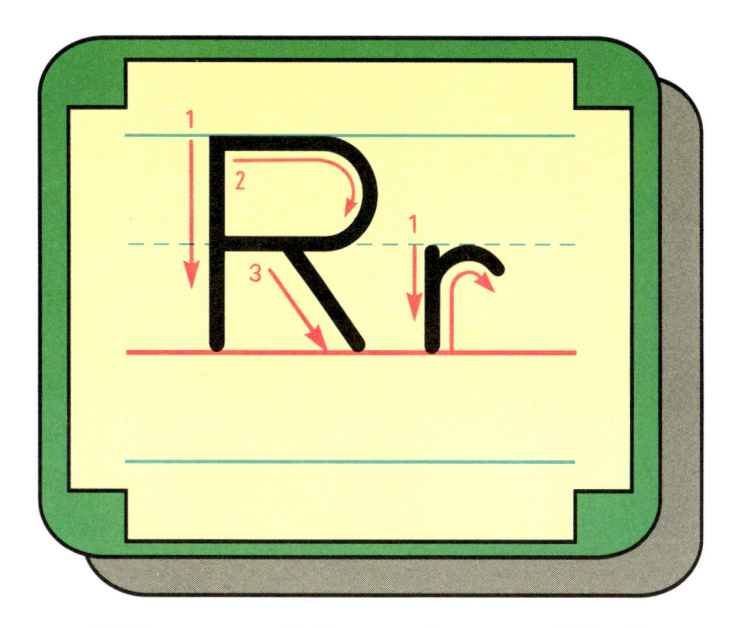

Three Men in a Tub

Rub-a-dub-dub,
Three men in a tub,
And how do you think they got there?
The butcher, the baker,
The candlestick-maker,
They all jumped out of a rotten potato,
'Twas enough to make a man stare.

Mother Goose

R r

62

Snowman

I want to make a snowman;
It's such a lot of fun
To roll and roll a snowball;
Don't spoil it, Mr. Sun.
Just stay behind that snow cloud,
And don't come out today.
I want to make a snowman,
So please don't spoil my day.

Unknown

S s

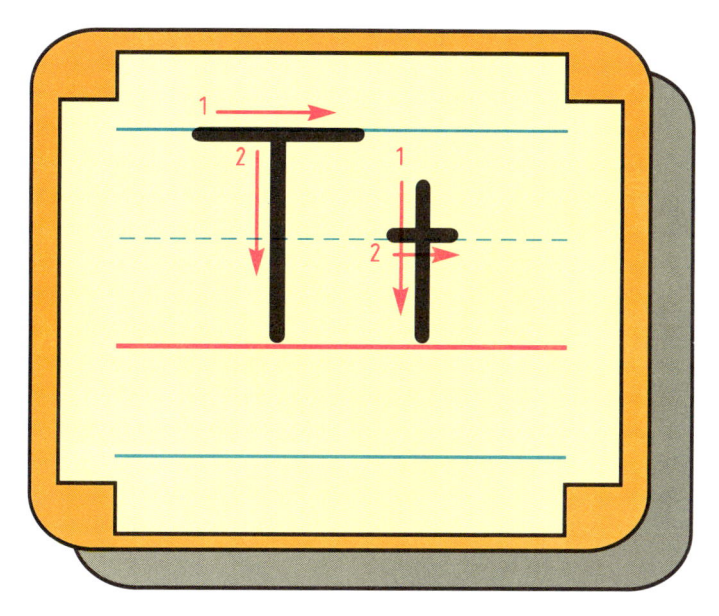

The Clock

With a tick and a tock,
And a tick and a tock,
The clock goes round all day.
It tells us when it's time to work,
And when it's time to play.

Unknown

T t

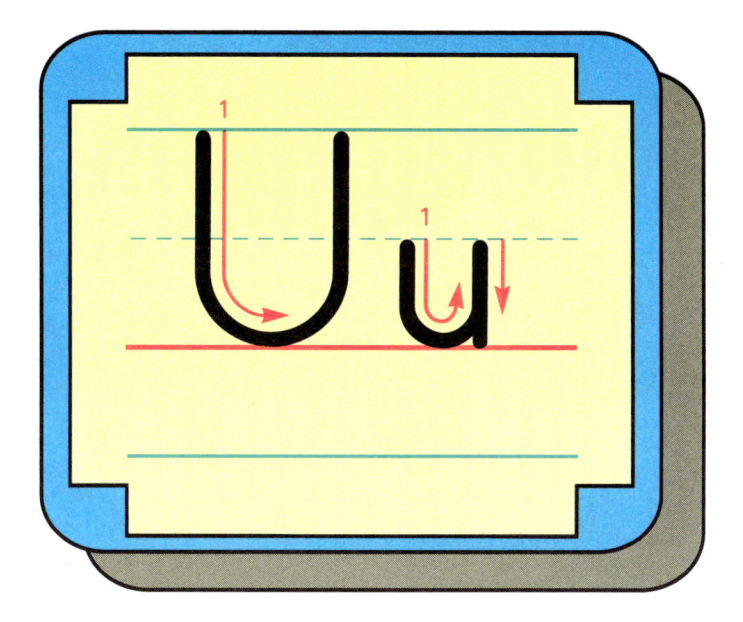

Umbrellas

Umbrellas bloom
Along our street
Like flowers on a stem.
And almost everyone
I meet
Is holding one of them.

Under my umbrella-top,
Splashing through the town,
I wonder why the tulips
Hold umbrellas
Up-side-down!

                Barbara Juster Esbensen

U   u

68
Copyright © Zaner-Bloser, Inc

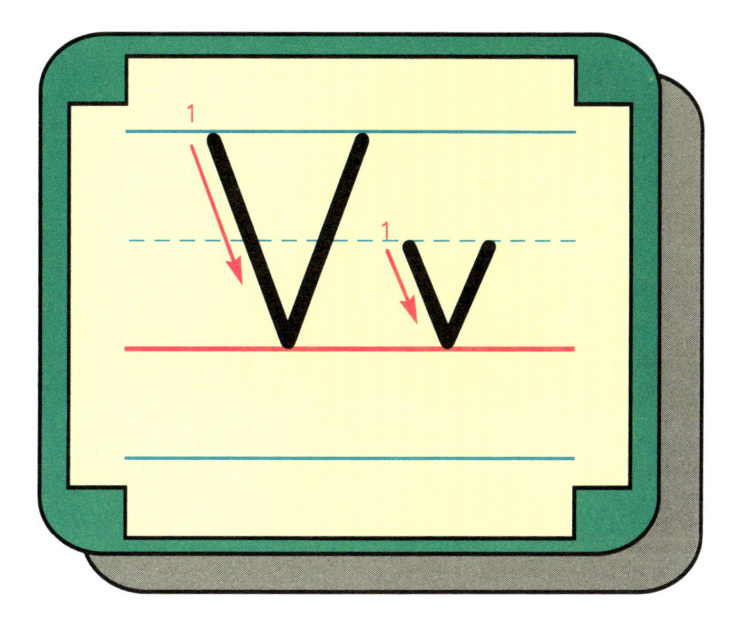

The Vulture

The Vulture eats between his meals
    And that's the reason why
He very, very rarely feels
    As well as you and I.

His eye is dull, his head is bald,
    His neck is growing thinner.
Oh! what a lesson for us all
    To only eat at dinner!

                    Hilaire Belloc

V v

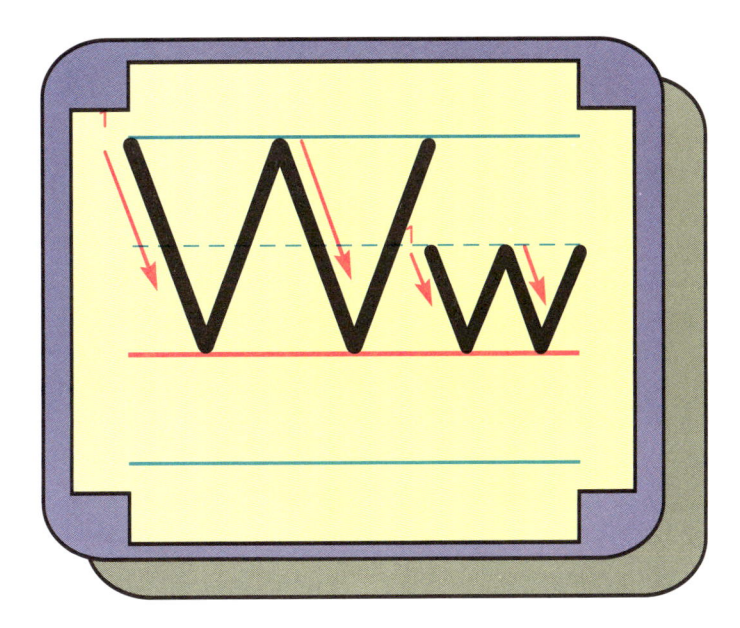

To Walk in Warm Rain

To walk in warm rain
    And get wetter and wetter!
To do it again—
To walk in warm rain
    Till you drip like a drain.
To walk in warm rain
    And get wetter and wetter.
            David McCord

Ww

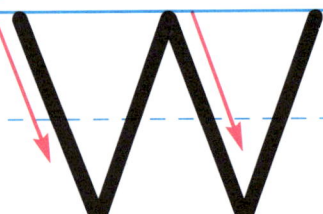

Jack in the Box

Jack in the box all shut up tight,
Not a breath of air,
Not a ray of light.
How tired he must be down in a heap,
We'll open the lid and up he will leap.

                    Unknown

X x

74

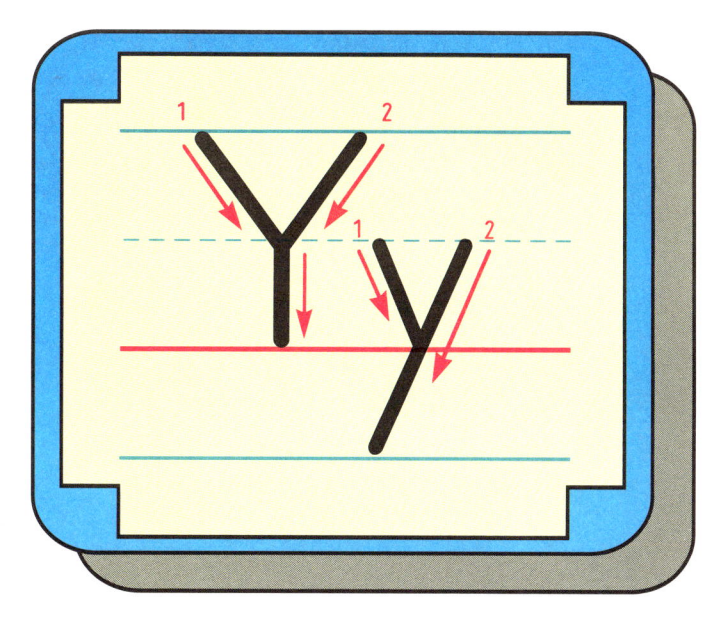

The Yak

Yickity-yackity, yickity-yak,
the yak has a scriffily, scraffily back;
some yaks are brown yaks and some yaks are black,
yickity-yackity, yickity-yak.

Sniggildy-snaggildy, sniggildy-snag;
the yak is all covered with shiggildy-shag;
he walks with a ziggildy-zaggildy-zag,
sniggildy-snaggildy, sniggildy-snag.

Yickity-yackity, yickity-yak,
the yak has a scriffily, scraffily back;
some yaks are brown yaks and some yaks are black,
yickity-yackity, yickity-yak.

Jack Prelutsky

Y y

76

My Zipper Suit

My zipper suit is bunny-brown—
The top zips up, the legs zip down.
I wear it every day.
My daddy brought it out from town.
Zip it up, and zip it down,
And hurry out to play!

                    Marie Louise Allen

Zach

Zoe Terlizzi
204 Zinc Lane
Zen, NJ 01100

Zebulon Zie
100 Zinnia Way
Zepplin, CA
00406

Z z

78 Copyright © Zaner-Bloser, Inc.

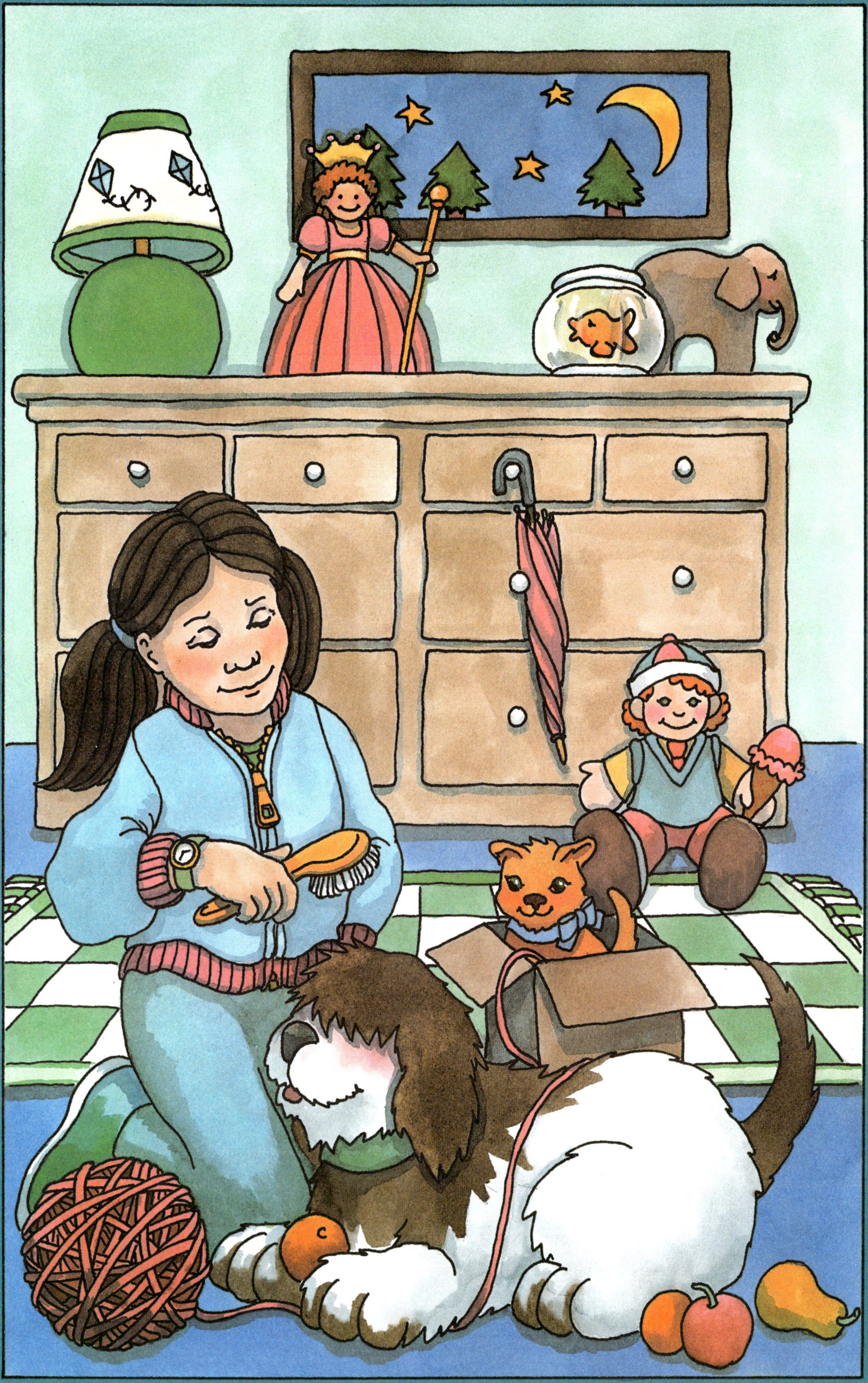

Match the uppercase and lowercase letters.

A ☐ B ☐ C ☐ D ☐ E ☐
F ☐ G ☐ H ☐ I ☐ J ☐
K ☐ L ☐ M ☐ N ☐ O ☐
P ☐ Q ☐ R ☐ S ☐ T ☐
U ☐ V ☐ W ☐ X ☐ Y ☐
Z ☐

a	j	d	m	b	h	e	c	l	k	i
f	g	p	x	y	s	o	v	q	w	z
n	r	t	u

Match the uppercase and lowercase letters.

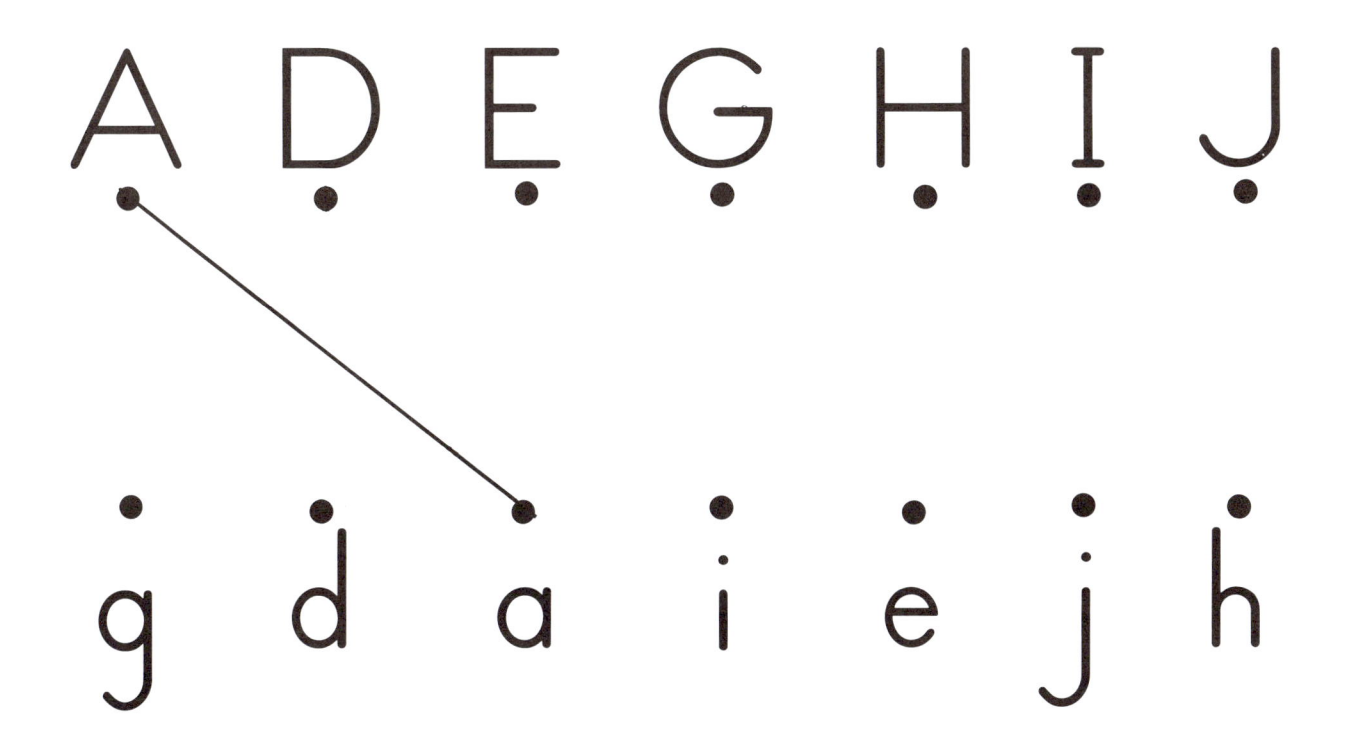

A D E G H I J

g d a i e j h

I N O Q R U Y

O L Q N R Y U

81

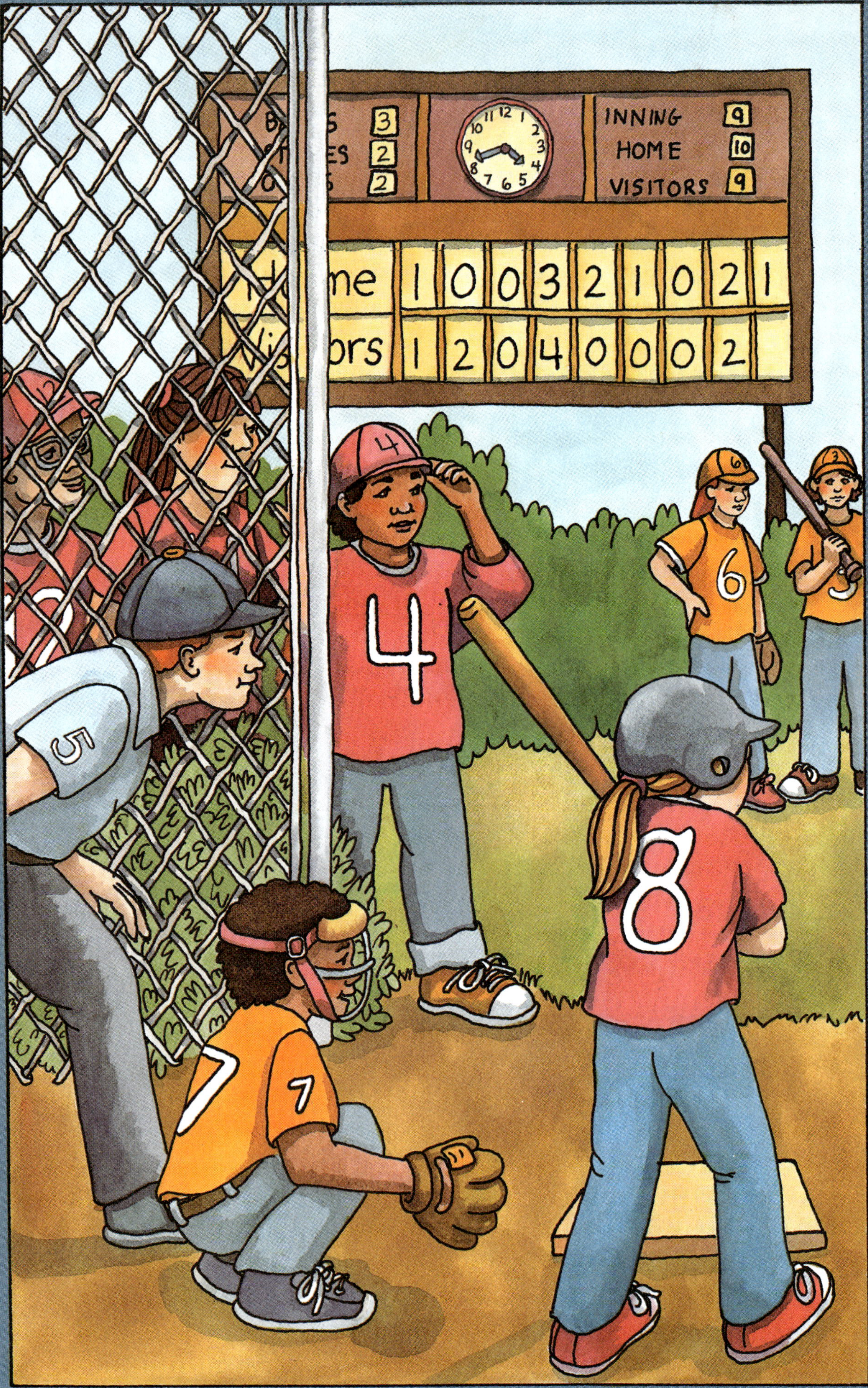
INNING 9
HOME 10
VISITORS 9

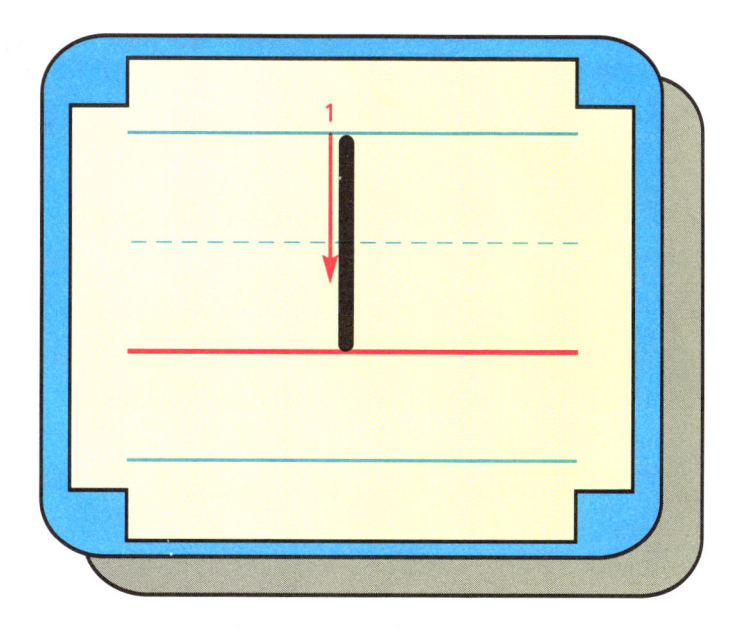

All of Me

See my eyes.
See my nose.
See my chin.
See my toes.
See my waist.
See my knee.
Now you have seen all of me!

                       Unknown

84

In the Apple Tree

Away up high in an apple tree
Two red apples smiled at me
I shook that tree as hard as I could
Down came the apples and m-m-m-m
   they were good.

> Unknown

2

Just Three

How very quiet things can be,
With just the dog, the cat, and me.
There's no one else to laugh and shout,
To dance and sing and run about.
With just the dog, the cat, and me,
How very quiet things can be.

William Wise

3

88
Copyright © Zaner-Bloser, Inc.

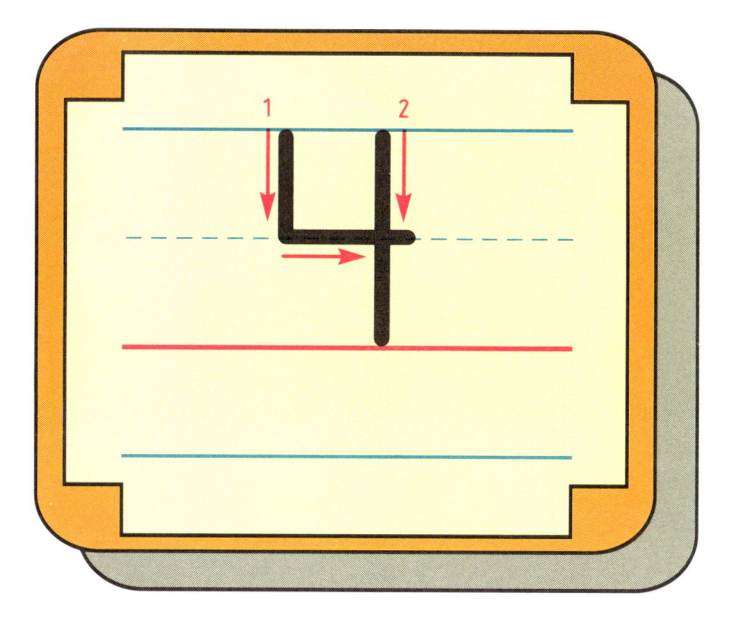

The Seasons

Spring is showery, flowery, bowery;
Summer: hoppy, croppy, poppy;
Autumn: wheezy, sneezy, freezy;
Winter: slippy, drippy, nippy.

                                Mother Goose

90

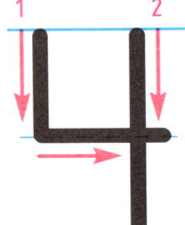

Five Baby Birds

Five baby birds in a nest in a tree
Are just as hungry as they can be.
"Peep," said baby bird number one.
Mother Bird promised she would come.
"Peep, peep," said baby bird number two.
If she doesn't come, what will we do?
"Peep, peep, peep," said baby bird
   number three.
I hope that she can find this tree.
"Peep, peep, peep, peep," said baby bird
   number four.
She never was so late before.
"Peep, peep, peep, peep, peep," said baby
   bird number five.
When will our mother bird arrive?
Well, here she comes to feed her family.
They're all as happy as they can be.

                                    Unknown

5

Birthday Candles

Today I have a birthday.
I'm six years old you see.
And here I have a birthday cake
Which you may share with me.
First we count the candles,
Count them, every one.
   One...two...three...four...
     five...six.
The counting now is done.
Let's snuff out the candles,
Out each flame will go...
   "wh...wh...wh...wh...
     wh...wh..."
As one by one we blow.

              Louise Binder Scott and
              J.J.Thompson

6

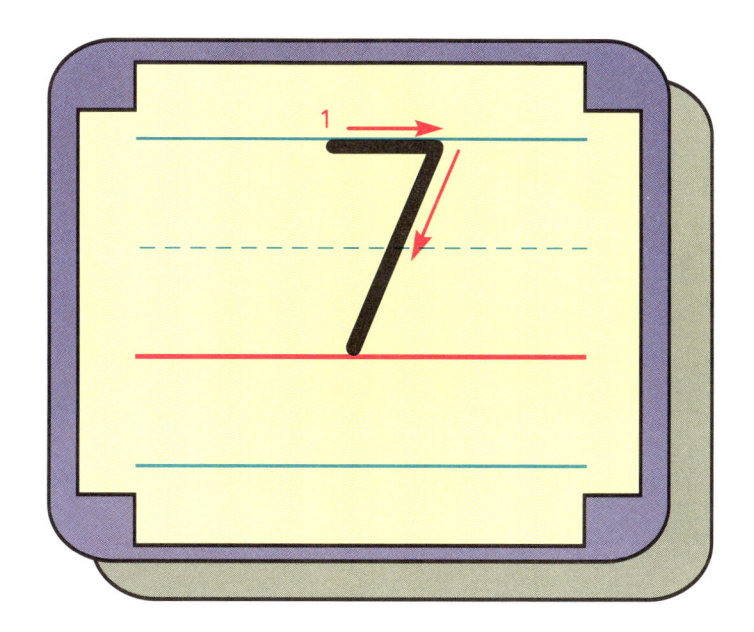

Going to St. Ives

As I was going to St. Ives
I met a man with seven wives.
Every wife had seven sacks,
Every sack had seven cats,
Every cat had seven kits.
Kits, cats, sacks, and wives,
How many were going to St. Ives?

Mother Goose

7

Eight Pigs

Two mother pigs lived in a pen,
Each had four babies and that made ten.
These four babies were black and white.
These four babies were black as night.
All eight babies loved to play.
And they rolled and they rolled in the
 mud all day.

                              Unknown

8

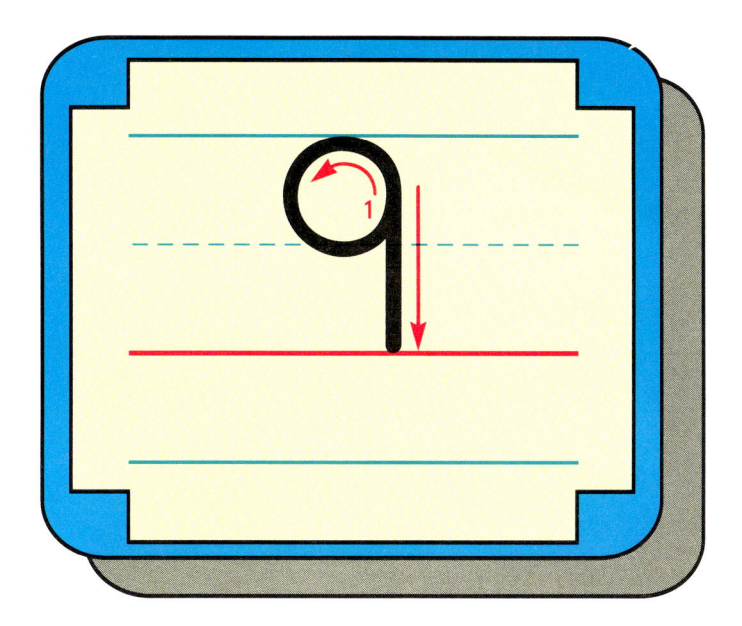

Pease Porridge

Pease porridge hot,
   Pease porridge cold,
Pease porridge in the pot,
   Nine days old.
Some like it hot,
   Some like it cold,
Some like it in the pot,
   Nine days old.

                Mother Goose

9

I Can Count

I can count. Want to see?
Here's my fingers. One, two, three,
Four and five. This hand is done.
Now I'll count the other one.
Six, seven, eight and nine.
Just one more. I'm doing fine.
The last little finger is number ten.
Now I'll count them all again.
One, Two, Three, Four, Five, Six,
   Seven, Eight, Nine, Ten.

Unknown

10

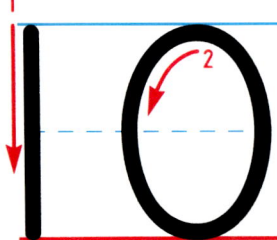

Connect the dots from 1 to 10.

My name is

I am

_____

years old.

I can

My telephone
number is

I live at

Music

1. Find some recordings of the songs Elizabeth, Mary and others might play on the pianoforte (e.g., the Italian songs and Scotch air played by Miss Bingley, p. 45).

2. Knowing what you do about Elizabeth's personality, what music do you think she would enjoy today? Make a tape for her and explain why she might like the music or how the lyrics might "speak" to her.

Research

1. Check one of many sources of information about Jane Austen on the Internet: http://uts.cc.utexas.edu/ churchh/ppjalmap.html

2. Find out more about the times in which the Bennet sisters lived. What was going on in the world? What fashions were being worn in England? Who was King? What inventions and discoveries were new? Give an illustrated talk that will provide readers with a better sense of the world these young women knew.

3. Prepare the menu Mrs. Bennet might have planned for a meal with which she hoped to impress one of her daughters' suitors. (Refer to vintage cookbooks.)

4. Do some research to find out which of the places in the novel are real and which are imaginary.

    (Real: Hertfordshire; Derbyshire—Blakewell, Chatsworth, Matlock, Dove Dale, the Peak, Blenheim, Oxford, Warwick, Kenilworth castle, Birmingham; Kent—Westerham, Ramsgate; Sussex-Brighton; London—Cheapside, Clapham; the Lake Country. Imaginary: Longbourn, Netherfield Park, Lucas Lodge, Meryton, Oakham Mount, Pemberley, Lambton, Kympton, Rosings, Hunsford)

Current Events

Create a bulletin board from newspaper and news magazine articles or ads that tie in with the novel in some way (e.g., a singles ad by someone who could be Lydia; a story about a gala that the Bennet sisters would have enjoyed attending; an article about con artists who prey on single women).

NOVEL UNITS © 1995 Anne Troy, Ph.D. and Phyllis Green, Ph.D.

Dance

Do a dance impression of a dramatic scene from the story, such as the scene where Darcy proposes to Elizabeth or where Elizabeth tells off Darcy's aunt.

Language Study

1. Have students make a list of epigrams found in the novel and star their favorite ones.

2. Have students list and explain allusions found in the novel.

3. List euphemisms found in the book and "translate" each into direct, blunt language.

4. Make a list of the 20 vocabulary words you think any reader of this novel should know—and why.

5. Make a list of 20 words used by Austen that are "dated" now—and provide their contemporary equivalents.

Art

1. Illustrate each character in the dress and pose you feel is most characteristic of each. For example, you might show Mrs. Bennet in her smartest outfit, shopping with a daughter for a wedding dress.

2. Capture your impressions of the Bennet family in a magazine cut-out collage.

3. Create a mobile based on the letters of correspondence and other objects in the novel. On the back of each object or hanging from it, write a brief explanation of the object's significance (e.g., Mr. Collins' letter to Mr. Bennet warning against a marriage between Elizabeth and Darcy).

4. Create a poster to advertise a movie version of the story.

5. Create a shoebox diorama of a scene from the story, such as Jane's being put to bed with a cold on her visit to the Bingleys'.

6. As a group project, use colored markers to illustrate a scene from the story on butcher paper.

novelists; *Jane Austen, the Woman*—a study of her life and environment based on primary sources such as published letters.

2. **Debate:** Debate some of the opinions expressed in the novel. For instance:
   - Think only of the past as its remembrance gives you pleasure.
   - We all love to instruct, though we can teach only what is not worth knowing.
   - You shouldn't marry for security if you're not in love.
   - If someone judges you by your family, that person isn't worth worrying about.

3. **Interview:** Pretend that Lydia, Jane, Elizabeth, Wickham, Bingley, and Darcy are appearing on a TV talk show about "when the man in your life deserves a second chance." Seven students role-play the part of the host and the six characters.) After the host briefly describes problems in each relationship, audience members address specific individuals. For example, "Lydia, don't you ever feel used by Wickham? You seem to care more about him than he does about you," and "Jane, don't you think Bingley is a bit of a wimp? Don't you ever get angry about the way he lets his best friend Darcy lead him around by the nose?"

Drama

1. Break into groups. Write and act out a favorite scene in the story (e.g., the scene where Darcy first proposes to Elizabeth or the scene where Elizabeth tells off Lady Catherine).

2. Write and act out a scene that is mentioned, but not directly shown, in the story—such as the scene where Lydia's uncle negotiates with Bingley about marrying his niece.

3. Write and act out a scene that might occur, but didn't. For example, show a scene during the time frame of the novel—e.g., the family celebrates Elizabeth's birthday (before her marriage—or after the final scene—e.g., Elizabeth brings her first child home to Grandma and Grandpa for a visit).

4. Stage and photograph several "tableaux" from the novel. Caption these "frozen shots" and create a bulletin board display.

f) Write an essay that begins with the topic sentence: "In the Bennets' world, social pressure, not individual choice, often determines marriages." Use evidence from the novel to develop your essay.

g) Consider the character of Elizabeth. Is she believable? Does she ever show poor judgment? What evidence is there that she undergoes a sharpening of self-knowledge? (You might want to refer to passages you marked P/S in pre-reading exercise #9.)

h) Compare and contrast two of the hypocrites in this story—Mr. Wickham and Mr. Collins. (How is their treatment of others similar? How is it different? What motivates each one?)

i) Choose one of the "anticipation guide" statements (prereading activity #1) and elaborate upon it—using evidence from the story to support your opinion.

j) What types of conflict do you find in this novel? What inner conflicts does Elizabeth undergo? With which other characters does she experience conflict? What are some examples of conflict with society?

k) What does *Pride and Prejudice* have to say about self-deception and self-knowledge? about how we choose our mates?

l) Jane Austen pokes fun at several follies surrounding courtship and marriage in the 1800's. Which of these "follies" are still common today?

Listening/Speaking
1. **Video:**
   a) Watch and discuss one of the film versions if you haven't already done so as a prereading activity. (How well do the actors convey the impressions you formed of Elizabeth, Jane, Mr. Darcy, etc. while reading the novel? What changes have been made in the movie? Why? For example, why do you think that in the movie Mr. Darcy's aunt was in favor of the match with Elizabeth?)

   b) Watch portions of the 5-part series, "Jane Austen and Her World" (Films for the Humanities, Inc., PO Box 2053, Princeton NJ; 800-257-5126)—24 minutes each. *Jane on a Summer's Day: Steventon Remembers*—a celebration of Austen's bi-centenary held in 1975 in her hometown. *The Keen, Bright Eye*—discussion of *Pride and Prejudice, Emma, Persuasion. Let Other Pens*—an analysis of Austen's view of the social scene and a discussion of its relevance in our time. *Jane Austen, the Novelist*—a discussion of problems encountered by

4. Write two or three items that might appear in the society column of the *Hertfordshire Herald* (or create your own title). (Look at your newspaper's society column for models of articles about engagements, weddings, anniversaries, social events, etc.)

5. Choose a character and write several entries in that character's dream diary.

6. Made-for-TV movie: Write the outline for a present-day version of *Pride and Prejudice* (about five sisters living today in your home town).

7. Retell a section of the story from Jane's point of view.

8. Write a letter of advice to Lydia, shortly before her marriage.

9. Write a "Dear Abby" letter from Elizabeth's or Mr. Bennet's point of view.

10. You are a marriage counselor who writes a monthly column in a women's magazine. You have interviewed Mr. and Mrs. Bennet or Mr. and Mrs. Wickham about their marriage. What problems do they have? Do you think their marriage can be "saved"? What advice do you have for this couple?

11. Write chapter titles for each chapter.

12. Review one of the film versions of the story. Include a brief summary of the story, evaluate changes made in the original, tell what you thought of the casting, and give an overall thumbs up or thumbs down.

Essay

a) Using *Bartlett's Quotations* or a similar reference, find a famous quote that somehow ties in with the story. Explain the connection.

b) Explain what Elizabeth values most. (Have her values changed over the course of the novel? Give evidence from the story for your answer.)

c) Compare and contrast Elizabeth, Jane, and Lydia. Which one do you think will have the happiest marriage? Why?

d) Choose a poem about love that somehow "speaks to" Jane Austen's novel. Compare what the poet is saying about love with what Austen seems to be saying in *Pride and Prejudice*.

e) Compare and contrast the sisters in this story with those in another one—*Little Women*.

Suggested Further Reading

Other Books by Jane Austen
   Emma, Mansfield Park, Persuasion, Sense and Sensibility, Northanger Abbey

Other Classics about Family Relationships/Romance
   Jane Eyre (Charlotte Bronte)
   Wuthering Heights (Emily Bronte)
   Little Women (Louisa May Alcott)
   David Copperfield (Dickens)
   Tess of the D'Urbervilles (Hardy)

Young Adult books about Family Relationships/Sisters/Romance
   Sebastian Sisters series (Susan Beth Pfeffer)
   Playing for Keeps (Kate Williams)
   Cecile (Janine Boissard)
   A Portrait of American Mothers and Daughters (Raisa Fastman)
   Shabanu, Daughter of the Wind (Suzanne Fisher Staples)

Viewing
Show students the videotape (90 minutes, color; call Novel Units for availability).

Writing
1. Write several of Elizabeth's journal entries—at different points in the story. (A partner might write journal entries that comment on the same situations—but from a different point of view, e.g. Mrs. Bennet's.)
2. Describe Bingley and Jane's wedding or Darcy and Elizabeth's. (Include the vows—written by themselves, perhaps.)
3. Write a poem in response to the novel. For example:
   - a diamente that describes how Elizabeth changes
   - a prayer poem spoken by Mrs. Bennet
   - a bitterness poem by Lady Catherine
   - a love poem by Jane, Elizabeth, Bingley, or Darcy
   - a poem of apology by Elizabeth
   - a poem that ends with a line taken from the story (e.g., "Happy for all her maternal feelings/ was the day on which Mrs. Bennet/got rid of her two most deserving daughters."

Post Reading Extension Activities

Post-Reading Discussion Questions

1. Did you find reading *Pride and Prejudice* more of a chore or a "delight"? Did your feelings about reading the book change as you got into it?

2. The diction and conventions of Jane Austen's prose reflect the manners, vocabulary, and values of her (19th century) society. Were you able to relate to this story? In what ways did you find the story "old-fashioned"? In what ways does it still "speak to" you, today?

3. If Jane and her sisters were alive today, what books would they like to read? What shows would they like to watch? What courses would they enjoy in school? What jobs would they choose? What vacations would they like? What would their hobbies and extracurricular activities be?

4. Is this a book that would appeal to men as well as women?

5. Suppose you were directing a "contemporized" version of *Pride and Prejudice*. Where would you set your story? Who would you cast? How would you modernize the story and update the characters' problems? Which character would you most like to play? Why?

6. What would you like to ask Jane Austen about the story? For example, what do you think she would say if asked how much of herself she "put into" the characters—and which ones?

7. Which of the characters change? Which are relatively flat and which are more rounded?

8. Which scenes from this story will you remember the longest? Which struck you as the funniest? Which reminded you of situations you have been in?

9. Did you see the movie? Did you use *Cliff's Notes*? What do you or don't you get from these that you get from reading the original text?

NOVEL UNITS © 1995 Anne Troy, Ph.D. and Phyllis Green, Ph.D.

The Author's Craft

Tone
Explain that the narrator's **tone** is her attitude toward a subject: serious, critical, laudatory, nostalgic, loving, etc.

Ask— How would you describe the narrator's tone in the following statement?
"Happy for all her maternal feelings was the day on which Mrs. Bennet got rid of her two most deserving daughters." (p. 321) (ironic)

How are readers expected to react to what the narrator is saying? (Mrs. Bennet is portrayed as a rather foolish, not terribly loving woman who is anxious to "get rid" of her daughters. Readers are expected to be amused.)

Epigram
In a letter to her sister, Jane Austen refers to the **epigrammatism** of her novel. Explain that an epigram is a pithy, concise saying. An epigram is often antithetical (balancing contrasts). For example: "Man proposes but God disposes."

Point out one or two epigrammatic passages in the book (e.g. Jane's advice to "Think only of the past as its remembrance gives your pleasure," p. 307, and the narrator's comment that Elizabeth was "resolving within herself to draw no limits in future to the impudence of an impudent man" p. 262).

Have students locate other examples.

12. How does Mrs. Bennet's attitude toward Darcy change? (She quickly accepts him when she learns that he has proposed.) Why? (She is happy about the prospect of Elizabeth's marrying into wealth.) How does Mr. Bennet's attitude change? Why? (He thinks better of Mr. Darcy when he learns that Elizabeth really loves him—and learns what Darcy has done to get Wickham to marry Lydia.)

13. How does Mr. Darcy explain falling in love with Elizabeth? (Long ago, he was struck by her "liveliness of mind" and by the affection she showed her sister.) Does this scene remind you of another scene—from a movie or another book you may have read?

14. What do you suppose Mr. Darcy writes in his letter to his aunt (p. 319)? (It tells of his engagement to Elizabeth.) What do you think Mr. Darcy's sister writes in her four-page response to the letter from him? (how happy she is about the match between Darcy and Elizabeth)

15. How do the marriages of Elizabeth and Jane affect their other family members? How does Mary benefit? (gets more attention from her parents) Kitty? (She benefits by spending more time with her older sisters and less with Lydia.) How does Mr. Bennet cope with missing Elizabeth's company? (visits often) Does Elizabeth help Lydia out? (sends some money) Does Lady Catherine get over Darcy's marriage to Elizabeth? (Elizabeth convinces her to reconcile; Lady Catherine condescends to visit—partly out of curiosity.)

16. **Prediction:** Do you think that Elizabeth is "good for" Darcy, and that Jane has a good influence on Bingley? How do you suppose the men will have changed after a few years of marriage? What about their wives?

Writing Activities

- Write the conversation that Bingley has with Jane right before asking Mr. Bennet for Jane's hand.

- Write the conversation that Bingley has with Mr. Bennet.

- When the sisters learned that Jane was to marry Bingley, "Mary petitioned for the use of the library at Netherfield; and Kitty begged very hard for a few balls there every winter" (p. 290). Write the dialogue.

5. Why has Mr. Collins written to Mr. Bennet about Elizabeth (p. 302)? (to advise against a match between Elizabeth and Darcy—as it would displease Lady Catherine) Why does Mr. Bennet think that the idea of a match between Elizabeth and Mr. Darcy is so absurd? (He has only heard Elizabeth speak negatively of Darcy.) Have you ever received unsolicited advice like this? How would you advise Mr. Bennet and his daughter to respond?

6. How does Elizabeth finally end up alone with Mr. Darcy (p. 304)? (He visits with Bingley; she takes a walk with him.) What is the first topic she brings up? (She thanks him for paying off Wickham's debts and getting him to marry Lydia.) What does this show you about her? (She expresses gratitude, even when it is awkward.) Why was Mr. Darcy so anxious to keep this matter secret? (He doesn't want her family to feel indebted to him.)

7. How do you suppose Elizabeth explained her change in feelings to Mr. Darcy?

8. How have the efforts of Mr. Darcy's aunt resulted in Elizabeth and Darcy's "present good understanding" (p. 305)?

Cause ⟶	Effect
Lady Catherine told Darcy that Elizabeth wouldn't promise to stay away from him.	Darcy realized he still had a chance with Elizabeth.

9. According to Mr. Darcy, how has Elizabeth changed him? (made him realize that he was being ungentlemanly, conceited, snooty) How does he fault his upbringing? (He was taught what was right, but as an only child was spoiled, selfish, and allowed to look down on others.)

10. Why has Mr. Bingley returned to Jane? (Mr. Darcy has given his okay.) What words do you suppose Mr. Darcy used when "confessing" his role in keeping Bingley and Jane apart? Is Bingley angry with his friend? (He wasn't happy to learn that Darcy kept the news from him that Jane was in London, but forgave him.) Would you be angry? How much influence does your best friend have over you when it comes to making other friends or developing romantic relationships?

11. How does Jane react at first when Elizabeth reveals her own engagement to Mr. Darcy? (surprised, reluctant) Why? (She isn't sure at first that Elizabeth is attracted to Darcy.)

Chapters 12-19
Pages 282-324 & Afterword

Vocabulary

indifferent 282	forbore 283	ceremonious 283	confederacy 284
rapacity 284	venison 285	haunch 285	concurrence 288
simpered 290	petitioned 290	barbarous 291	shift 292
equipage 292	hermitage 294	insolent 294	industriously 295
allurements 295	tacit 296	dissuaded 297	brooking 297
upstart 297	recede 297	frivolous 298	incensed 298
wavering 300	appeased 301	sagacity 301	precipitate 302
diverted 302	abominate 303	hypocrisy 303	diffused 305
denoted 306	irrevocably 306	premises 306	annexed 306
devoid 306	quest 309	unabated 309	incredulous 310
grandeur 313	assiduously 317	moralize 322	arrear 323

Discussion Questions

1. Elizabeth asks herself, "Is there one among the [male] sex who would not protest against such a weakness as a second proposal to the same woman? There is no indignity so abhorrent to their feelings" (p. 284). What is she thinking? (No man would risk rejection twice.) Do you agree? Do you think that in relationships today, it is still men who risk rejection more often than women?

2. Why does Elizabeth tell Jane, "We all love to instruct, though we can teach only what is not worth knowing"? Do you agree? (Elizabeth wants Jane to see that Bingley still loves her; Jane has to see it for herself.)

3. What do you suppose Bingley and Mr. Bennet say to each other about Elizabeth (p. 289)? (Bingley asks for her hand, says he loves her.) Do you think either has any qualms about the engagement?

4. Why does Lady Catherine de Bourgh pay a call on the Bennets? (to insist that Elizabeth not get involved with Darcy) Does she accomplish her purpose? (no) Is Elizabeth rude to her? Which of her "come-backs" do you think were the best ones? How would Jane have responded if Lady Catherine had spoken this way to her?

13. Why is Elizabeth so miserable when Mr. Darcy and Mr. Bingley pay a visit to the Bennets (p. 281)? (Her mother is cordial to Mr. Bingley, but cold to Mr. Darcy—to whom she unknowingly owes a great debt.) Is Mrs. Bennet being rude? What would you do if you felt that your parents were being rude to your friends?

14. **Prediction:** Will Mrs. Bennet's opinion of Mr. Darcy ever change? Will Elizabeth reveal what she knows about Mr. Darcy's getting Wickham to marry Lydia?

Writing Activity

- Write the letter Mr. Bennet sends to Mr. Gardiner in response to Mr. Gardiner's explanation of Lydia's marriage settlement. (p. 257)
- When Elizabeth thinks that she has lost Mr. Darcy, she realizes that many of his qualities would complement her own (p. 259). "She began to comprehend that he was exactly the man who, in disposition and talents, would most suit her." Describe the person who would "suit" you ideally—and how your qualities—good and bad—would complement that person's.

The Author's Craft: Euphemism

Explain that a **euphemism** is a figure of speech in which an indirect statement is substituted for a direct one in an effort to avoid bluntness. Point out that the narrators and many of the characters use euphemisms, whereas Elizabeth often says exactly what is on her mind. Have students look at the description of Mr. Wickham and Elizabeth (p. 274), following the conversation in which she lets him know that she is aware of what really happened between him and Darcy:

> "Mr. Wickham was so perfectly satisfied with this conversation that he never again distressed himself, or provoked his dear sister Elizabeth, by introducing the subject of it; and she was pleased to find that she had said enough to keep him quiet."

Have students describe Wickham's reaction in more blunt, accurate language. (Wickham knew that Elizabeth had called his bluff, and he didn't dare bring the subject up again.)

What is the effect of contrasting euphemism and blunt language here? (The author is emphasizing that while Wickham is self-serving and hypocritical, Elizabeth sees and calls things as they are, not as society dictates.)

6. How does Mrs. Bennet react when she learns that Lydia is to be married? (excited) Is she grateful for all that her brother has done? (She says it is the least he can do.) Is Mr. Bennet grateful? (He worries about having to repay his brother-in-law.) What sort of disagreement arises concerning Lydia's future residence? (Mrs. Bennet wants her well set-up, close by; Mr. Bennet says she will not be welcome in his home anymore.) With whom do you side in this argument—Mr. or Mrs. Bennet?

7. Why is Jane so miserable on Lydia's wedding day? (She assumes that Lydia feels guilty and embarrassed.) Have you ever been in a situation where you felt more distressed for someone than he felt for himself? Do you think Lydia should have acted more apologetic?

8. Does Elizabeth decide that Wickham loves Lydia? (no) What does she conclude about his reasons for running off with her? (She assumes he ran away from gambling debts and took Lydia along for fun.) Do you think Elizabeth ever tells Lydia how she feels about Wickham? Should she? Do you think Lydia's feelings for Wickham will change?

9. Why is Elizabeth amazed by Lydia's description of her wedding day? (Lydia reveals that Darcy was there.) Why does Elizabeth write to her aunt instead of getting an explanation from her sister? (Lydia says Darcy has asked for secrecy.) Do you think Elizabeth knows already what she will learn? Do you ever try to "pry secrets" out of someone—or do you think secrets should be respected?

10. Why is Elizabeth's aunt so surprised to get the letter from her niece? (She assumes Elizabeth knew what Darcy had done—and had done it for Elizabeth.) What does Mrs. Gardiner reveal about her husband's role in securing Lydia's marriage? (He didn't put up the money.) What does she mean, "...your letter gave him great pleasure, because it required an explanation that would rob him of his borrowed feathers" (p. 270)? (He didn't want the Bennets to think he was the one who had paid Darcy.)

11. How does the knowledge of what Mr. Darcy has done for the Bennets affect Elizabeth? (She is moved, puzzled, happy that he may still be in love with her, upset that he may not give her a second chance after this humiliating family episode.) Have you ever been in a situation like hers where you felt happy and pained at the same time?

12. In what tone of voice do you imagine Mr. Bennet saying, "I defy even Sir William Lucas himself to produce a more valuable son-in-law" (p. 275)? (ironic) What is Mr. Bennet's real opinion of Wickham? (that he his a self-serving jerk)

Chapters 6-11
Pages 244-281

Vocabulary

dilatory 244	intimates 245	heinous 247	perplexity 248
paddock 250	per annum 251	explicitly 252	complied 252
pledged 255	calico 255	muslin 255	cambric 255
transports 257	indolence 257	proportionate 257	nuptials 257
guinea 258	gulf 259	alliance 259	spurned 259
corps 260	austerity 262	compatible 266	confidante 266
copse 267	expedite 268	abhorrence 271	palatable 274
canvassed 276	etiquette 277	intervene 277	indebted 278

Discussion Questions

1. Why is it that Mrs. Gardiner is a great comfort to the Bennets in their time of trouble while Mrs. Phillips is not (p. 244)? (Mrs. Gardiner is sensible and reassuring; Mrs. Phillips is a gossip who sharpens their anxieties by bringing up ever more bad news about Wickham.)

2. What motive do you think Mr. Collins has for writing to the Bennets (p. 246)? (to "rub it in" that their family is in disgrace)

3. Why is Elizabeth shocked to hear that Wickham is a "gamester"? What is that? (gambler; Wickham is in debt.)

4. What is ironic about Mrs. Bennet's cry when she learns that her husband is returning home, "Who is to fight Wickham...?" What had she said earlier? (She had professed concern for Mr. Bennet's safety when he was gone lest he get into a fight, be killed, and leave her and the girls penniless.) Do you think she loves her husband? Is Mr. Bennet sympathetic toward his wife when he comes home and finds her holed up in her room? (He makes a sarcastic comment about her sitting in her nightcap, being waited on.)

5. Why does Mr. Gardiner write to Mr. Bennet "you will easily comprehend from these particulars that Mr. Wickham's circumstances are not so hopeless as they are generally believed to be" (p. 251)? (Wickham, surprisingly, has not asked for much money.) What does Elizabeth assume Mr. Gardiner has left out of the letter? (that he has discharged the debts, himself) What do you think would have happened if Mr. Gardiner hadn't found Wickham and Lydia?

Mr. Darcy? (He happens to come in as she is reading the bad news.) Is he understanding? (yes; He blames himself for not revealing Wickham's true nature to all.) Why does she help write notes with "false excuses for their sudden departure" (p. 233)? (to keep everyone from finding out about Lydia's dishonor)

7. Why didn't Elizabeth tell Lydia what she knew about Mr. Wickham's running off with Mr. Darcy's sister? (She didn't foresee that Lydia was in danger as Wickham hadn't shown Lydia special attention up to this point; Mr. Darcy had told her in confidence.) Do you think that would have altered Lydia's behavior toward Wickham?

8. Who does Mrs. Bennet blame for Lydia's conduct? (the Colonel's wife, for not supervising Lydia) How does she feel the situation could have been avoided? Who does the narrator think is ultimately to blame? (Lydia's parents)

9. Why does Mr. Gardiner go to London? (to find Lydia and Wickham) What else could the family do, under the circumstances? Do you think Lydia realizes how upset her family must be? Why does Elizabeth say, "under such a misfortune as this, one cannot see too little of one's neighbors" (p. 243) (The family didn't want gossip to start.) Do you "care what the neighbors think" about your family?

10. **Prediction:** Will Lydia and Wickham be married?

Writing Activity

In conversation with Mr. Darcy, Miss Bingley criticizes Elizabeth out of anger and jealousy. The narrator points out that "this was not the best method of recommending herself; but angry people are not always wise" (p. 225). Write a dialogue in which anger leads someone to say something unwise.

The Author's Craft: Characterization

Explain that **characterization** is the way an author informs readers about what characters are like. **Direct characterization** is when the author describes the character. **Indirect characterization** is when the reader figures out what the character is like based on what the character thinks, says, or does—or what other characters say about him or her.

<u>Ask students</u>—What is Mr. Darcy like, according to the housekeeper? Do you think she is a reliable observer? Up until now, how have we formed our impressions of Mr. Darcy? (From the narrator's description of his behavior, as well as perceptions of Elizabeth and others, we have seen a proud, arrogant man.) How does our view of Mr. Darcy change as we begin to see him through this "new" pair of eyes? (It improves; she insists that he is good-tempered and generous, a good landlord and master.)

Volume 3
Chapters 1-5
Pages 203-244

Vocabulary

perturbation 203	proprietor 204	arrested 208	trifling 208
adorned 210	revolted 211	decamping 212	acceded 213
embargo 213	curricle 216	livery 216	discomposure 216
cordiality 217	predominate 223	disengaged 224	saloon 225
shrewish 225	turnpikes 228	impetuous 229	commiseration 229
alluded 229	eloped 229	acquiescence 230	contracted 230
palliation 230	unavailing 231	indulgence 232	deranged 232
postscript 233	hackney 234	expeditiously 234	quartered 235
extravagant 236	lamentations 238	invectives 238	indulgence 238
spasms 239	prudence 240	fretfulness 240	irretrievable 240

Discussion Questions

1. According to the housekeeper, what are Mr. Darcy's good points? (generous, kind) How do you explain the fact that her view of Mr. Darcy is so different from Elizabeth's?

2. How is Mr. Darcy's behavior changed when he meets Elizabeth at Pemberley? (He is very civil.) Are they happy to see each other, do you think?

3. How do Mr. Darcy and the Gardiners get along? (well) Why is Mr. Darcy surprised that they are Elizabeth's relations? (The Gardiners are sensible, well-spoken, unlike the rest of her foolish family.)

4. How does Elizabeth feel about being introduced to Mr. Darcy's sister? (surprised, gratified that he still regards her highly enough to want Georgiana to meet her) How is Miss Darcy different from what Elizabeth had expected? (shy, not conceited as Mr. Wickham had said) Do you think that shy people are often mistakenly thought to be stuck up or aloof?

5. Why is Miss Bingley jealous of Elizabeth? (Miss Bingley knows that Darcy still has his eye on Elizabeth.) How does that jealousy show itself? (She criticizes every aspect of Elizabeth's appearance and personality.) Does Elizabeth realize how Miss Bingley feels about her, do you think?

6. Why does Jane write, asking Elizabeth to return? (Lydia has run off with Wickham.) Why does the family want Lydia to marry Mr. Wickham? (to preserve the family's reputation) Why does Elizabeth confide about her family's troubles to

NOVEL UNITS © 1995 Anne Troy, Ph.D. and Phyllis Green, Ph.D.

6. Why do Elizabeth and Jane decide not to tell what they know about Wickham's true character? (They don't think anyone would believe it and he'll be gone soon, anyway.) Would you?

7. Why does Elizabeth advise her father not to let Lydia go to Brighton? (She thinks Lydia will get into trouble by partying, unsupervised.) Is she more worried about Lydia—or herself? (She does think about how Lydia's behavior will reflect on the family.) What pros and cons do you suppose Mr. and Mrs. Bennet weigh? Why do you think they let her go, in the end? (Mr. Bennet finds it easier to give in.) Who do you think is more mature—Mrs. Bennet or Elizabeth?

8. On the regiment's last day in Meryton, how does Wickham treat Elizabeth? (charmingly) Why does he start to renew his attentions to her—but part from her a short time later with a "mutual desire of never meeting again" (p. 197)? (She lets him know that she knows his true nature and his past.)

9. What sort of marriage do Mr. and Mrs. Bennet have? (no real affection) What does the narrator mean, "Elizabeth...had never been blind to the impropriety of her father's behavior as a husband" (p. 198)? (She knows that her father doesn't respect her mother.)

10. What invitation have the Gardiners extended to Elizabeth? (go on a tour with them) Who will watch their children? (Jane) What route do they take? (Hertfordshire to Derbyshire, taking in Blenheim, Oxford, Warwick, Birmingham) How does Elizabeth feel about going to Pemberley? (nervous that she will run into Darcy; curious) Do you think she secretly hopes to see Mr. Darcy?

11. **Prediction:** Will Elizabeth meet Mr. Darcy while viewing Pemberley?

Writing Activity
Reread the first paragraph of Chapter 19 ("Had Elizabeth's opinion been all drawn from her own family, she could not have formed a very pleasing picture of conjugal felicity..."). Write a flashback portraying the early days of Elizabeths' parents' courtship. Show some of the qualities that attracted Mr. and Mrs. Bennet to each other.

The Author's Craft
Explain that a **paradox** is a statement which, while seemingly contradictory or absurd, may actually be well-founded or true. Point out the example on page 200:
"Mrs. Bennet was restored to her usual querulous serenity."
"Querulous" means complaining and "serenity" means composure or peacefulness. While it may seem that someone who is always complaining could not be considered peaceful, this is as close as Mrs. Bennet comes to composure—closer than she had been when Lydia first went away.

Chapters 11-19
Pages 159-202

Vocabulary

degradation 160	abominable 164	verdure 165	dissipation 170
penitent 172	affinity 173	perturbed 173	profligacy 173
militia 174	mediocrity 175	discernment 176	obeisance 177
diminution 178	discreditable 179	upbraided 179	repent 179
chagrin 180	indecorum 180	indispensably 180	domestics 181
hitherto 182	liberal 185	retailing 186	enumerating 186
depreciate 187	plague 187	vindication 188	lament 189
tumult 190	incumbrance 190	fervently 191	imprudent 194
aloof 194	volatility 194	amendment 194	augment 195
volubility 195	affectation 195	imputed 197	grievances 197
adieus 198	conjugal 198	minutely 199	
parasol 199	querulous 200		

Discussion Questions

1. How does Elizabeth react to Mr. Darcy's proposal? (turns him down flatly) Why does she feel insulted? (He says he is proposing against his own better judgment, that her family is inferior.)

2. Why do you think Darcy writes Elizabeth a letter instead of speaking with her? How does he defend himself in the letter? (says that he was protecting his friend because he didn't think that Jane really loved Bingly; that Wickham actually squandered his inheritance and wronged Darcy by running off with his sister) Why does he suggest that she talk with Col. Fitzwilliam? (to confirm his negative view of Wickham) Do you think he is being honest with her? with himself? Does the letter change how she feels about him?

3. Does Elizabeth feel that Mr. Darcy's criticisms of her family are justified? (She knows that her family can be foolish.) What would he think of your family?

4. Why does Lydia want her parents to take the family to Brighton for the summer? (That is where the militia will be.) What is her "good news" about Wickham? (Wickham isn't going to marry Miss King after all.)

5. What is Jane's reaction to Elizabeth's revelation that Mr. Darcy has proposed? (shocked, feels sorry for Mr. Darcy) Does she blame Elizabeth for refusing him? (says no) Should Elizabeth tell her what she knows about Darcy's role in separating Jane and Bingley?

12. How do Charlotte and Elizabeth explain the frequent visits Mr. Darcy pays to Elizabeth? (Charlotte thinks he is interested in Elizabeth; both agree that Darcy may be bored at his aunt's.) One topic Elizabeth and Darcy discuss is living near family after marriage. Do you think that it is preferable to live near your family after you marry? What else do Elizabeth and Darcy talk about? (the departure of Bingleys' party from Netherfield)

13. How does Elizabeth learn that Mr. Darcy influenced his friend, Bingley, to stop seeing Jane? (Col. Fitzwilliam tells her.) What do you think Mr. Darcy's motives were?

14. **Prediction:** Do you think Elizabeth will tell Jane what she has learned? Will she confront Darcy?

Writing Activities
- Elizabeth and Charlotte corresponded after Charlotte's wedding. Write one of these letters.
- Describe a time when something happened to cool your friendship with someone. You continued to be friends—but things were never the same again.

The Author's Craft: Point of View

Explain that the **point of view** is the vantage point from which the author tells the story—through whose eyes the story is told. There are two basic ways an author may present the events in the story: first person narrator ("I") or third person narrator ("he" or "she"). Point out that the narrator is not necessarily speaking for the author.

Ask—from whose point of view is this story told? (third person) What kind of person is the narrator? Is he or she reliable, do you think? (polite, well acquainted with the kinds of people she writes about, a close observer of human nature)

5. When does Jane finally see the light about Miss Bingley—that Miss Bingley is really no friend of hers? (when Miss Bingley gives her the cold shoulder in London) Why do you suppose Miss Bingley acted so friendly at first? Has anyone ever treated you like this?

6. Why does Mr. Wickham's attention to Elizabeth cool? (She doesn't offer him wealth; Miss King comes into an inheritance.) Is Elizabeth angry about it? (no) Should she be? Do you think Charlotte's acceptance of Mr. Collins is like Mr. Wickham's attentions to Miss King? Does Jane see a similarity?

7. What plans does Elizabeth make for a trip to see Charlotte? (She will accompany Charlotte's father and sister in the spring.) How does she enjoy the visit? (She enjoys visiting Charlotte, but has to put up with Mr. Collins and visits to snooty Lady Catherine.) Is she uncomfortable around Mr. Collins? Would you find this an awkward situation?

8. How does Elizabeth first meet Miss De Bourgh? (Mr. Collins accepts an invitation to dine with Lady Catherine.) "She looks sickly and cross. Yes, she will do for him very well. She will make him a very proper wife." (p. 136) What is Elizabeth thinking? (She has heard that Darcy is expected to marry young Miss De Bourgh. Elizabeth feels happy that Darcy's intended looks unwell and unpleasant.)

9. Why is Mr. Collins so happy to get the invitation to Rosings? (He takes every opportunity to ingratiate himself to his patronness.) Does Elizabeth enjoy the visit? (She keeps her sense of humor.) Would you? What is Elizabeth's opinion of Lady Catherine? (cold, self-important, affected) What is the narrator's opinion? (She is satirizing Lady Catherine's type.)

10. Why does Mr. Darcy show up at the parsonage? (to visit Elizabeth) Is Elizabeth happy to see him? (surprised) Does he seem happy to see her? (doesn't show it) Do you think Elizabeth is attracted to Mr. Darcy's cousin, Col. Fitzwilliam? (somewhat) Do you think there is a sense of rivalry between the cousins? (Darcy does come over when Fitzwilliam asks Elizabeth to play piano.) Why do you suppose Col. Fitzwilliam doesn't pursue Elizabeth further? (She isn't a woman of fortune.)

11. What offer does Mr. Darcy's aunt make to Elizabeth? (She can come over and play the piano.) Do you think Elizabeth is insulted by the offer? (yes) Why does she tell Darcy "my courage always rises with every attempt to intimidate me" (p. 148)? (He is standing where he can watch her play, which she sees as an attempt to interfere with her playing.) Do you think he is trying to intimidate her?

Volume 2
Chapters 1-10
Pages 115-159

Vocabulary

caprice 116	repine 116	extenuating 120	alleviated 120
artful 121	commendation 123	duped 128	defection 129
dejection 131	mercenary 131	discretion 131	effusions 133
parsonage 133	pales 133	tenor 135	apparel 137
formidable 138	trepidation 138	composedly 138	controverted 140
gig 143	sallied 144	disclaim 145	counterbalance 154
patronage 154	rencontre 155	inured 156	prodigious 157
tractable 157	surmise 158		

Discussion Questions

1. How does Jane feel when she gets the letter from Miss Bingley (p. 115)? (crushed) Why do you suppose there is so much talk about Miss Darcy in the letter? (Miss Bingley wants to let Jane know that someone has taken her place in Bingley's heart.) Is Jane angry that Mr. Bingley appears to have dumped her? (no) Should she be? Do you agree with her that "women fancy admiration means more than it does" (p. 118)?

2. What is the contrast between Jane's and Elizabeth's views of Charlotte's marriage to Mr. Collins? (Jane thinks Charlotte is being practical; Elizabeth is disappointed in her best friend.) With which one do you agree? Do you think that Jane is too much of a Pollyanna—or is Elizabeth too cynical?

3. Who is Mrs. Gardiner? (the wife of Mrs. Bennet's brother) Why is she a favorite with her nieces? (She is young, amiable, intelligent.) Why does she invite Jane to London? (She learns from Elizabeth of Jane's broken heart.) Is she trying to get Jane and Bingley back together? Would you like her as an aunt?

4. Why does Mrs. Gardiner advise Elizabeth against getting involved with Wickham? (He has no money.) Is Elizabeth influenced by Mrs. Gardiner's opinion? (She respects her aunt, but doesn't promise to drop Wickham.) Does she mind her aunt's "butting in"? Would you?

6. Are Elizabeth's parents both disappointed by her turning Mr. Collins down? (just her mother) Do you think Elizabeth would have changed her mind if her father had insisted? Why do you suppose Elizabeth is her father's favorite daughter—but "the least dear to her [mother] of all her children"? Do most parents have a favorite child?

7. What happens to chill the friendship between Elizabeth and Charlotte? (Charlotte accepts Mr. Collins's proposal.) Do you think Charlotte has let Elizabeth down? Has she let herself down? Why does she accept him? (material security) Why did Mr. Collins set his sights on Charlotte—and so soon after his rejection by Elizabeth? Is this a case of "catching someone on the rebound"?

8. Why does the letter from Miss Bingley upset Jane? (Miss Bingley reveals that the entire party—including her brother—has gone to London and does not plan to return.) How do Elizabeth and Jane read the letter differently? (Elizabeth reads between the lines that Bingley's sisters are trying to break things up between Bingley and Jane; Jane thinks that Miss Bingley is merely trying to warn her that Bingley has fallen out of love with her.) Which one do you suppose is closer to the truth?

9. Why does Mrs. Bennet now regard Charlotte with "jealous abhorrence" (p. 112)? (As Mr. Collins' wife, Charlotte will one day inherit the Bennets' estate.) In what tone of voice do you imagine Mr. Bennet saying, "...Let us flatter ourselves that I may be the survivor"? (sarcastic) Does Mrs. Bennet respond to the feelings underneath her husband's words? (no)

10. **Prediction:** Will Mr. Bingley and Jane ever get together?

Writing Activity
It is the evening after the Netherfield ball. Write journal entries from the points of view of Elizabeth, Jane, Mr. Bingley, Mr. Darcy, and Mr. Collins.

The Author's Craft: Theme
Explain that a **theme** is a general truth or commentary on life brought out through a literary work. Often the title and recurring incidents or phrases are a clue to the theme of a novel. Tell students to pay special attention to characters' conversations about "pride" and "prejudice." What does Elizabeth say to Mr. Darcy about prejudice on page 81? What might the author's message about prejudice be? (Elizabeth points out that for a person who is rigid in his or her judgments of others, it is particularly important not to be blinded by prejudice when first forming those opinions.)

Chapters 18-23
Pages 77-113

Vocabulary

mortification 78	taciturn 79	éclat 79	hauteur 79
allusion 80	unappeasable 81	prejudice 81	steward 82
complacency 82	conditionally 83	discourse 83	patroness 84
laity 84	contempt 85	perverseness 86	animating 86
vexation 86	gravity 87	entreaties 87	conciliatory 88
manoeuvre 89	repulsed 89	eclipsed 90	injunction 91
incessant 91	disservice 91	composure 91	vivacity 92
sanctioned 95	vestibule 95	felicitations 95	estimation 99
peevish 99	abatement 99	forbearance 100	partiality 102
desponding 104	conjecture 105	diffident 105	irksome 106
courtier 109	vent 110	rectitude 111	abode 111

Discussion Questions

1. Why isn't Mr. Wickham at the Netherfield ball? (He's avoiding Darcy.) Is Elizabeth disappointed? (yes) Have you ever been in a situation like hers?

2. Do Mr. Darcy and Elizabeth enjoy dancing with each other? (Their conversation is awkward.) Why do you think Mr. Darcy looks over at Bingley and Jane—who are dancing together—"with a very serious expression" (p. 80)? What do you suppose he is thinking?

3. What does Miss Bingley tell Elizabeth about Mr. Wickham? (that Wickham has treated Darcy badly) What do you think Miss Bingley's motives are? After all, doesn't she have a better chance with Mr. Darcy if Elizabeth stays interested in Mr. Wickham?

4. How does Mrs. Bennet embarrass Elizabeth? (by talking loudly of Jane's prospects for marrying Bingley) How does Mary embarrass Elizabeth? (by singing poorly, with affectation) What would you do if you were Elizabeth? Have you ever been in a situation like hers?

5. How does Elizabeth turn down Mr. Collins? (She tells him flatly that he could not make her happy.) Why? What else could she have said—and done? Is Mr. Collins crushed? (He assumes she will change her mind.) Is there anything Mr. Collins—or anyone else—could have said or done to convince Elizabeth to change her mind?

9. Why does Mrs. Bennet's opinion of Mr. Collins change? (She had disliked him because of the inheritance; now she thinks he would make a good catch for one of her daughers.) Does she think that Elizabeth could be happy with Mr. Collins? (She probably doesn't think much about that; her motives are financial ones.) What would you have advised Elizabeth to say to her mother about Mr. Collins, if she were your friend? Why is Mrs. Bennet so eager to marry off her daughters? Do you think this is still a major concern of parents today?

10. Who is Mr. Wickham? (charming new member of the corps) What does Elizabeth think of him? (She finds him handsome, easy to converse with.) How can she tell that there is tension between Mr. Darcy and Mr. Wickham? (Darcy didn't return Wickham's greeting.) According to Mr. Wickham, what is the source of the tension? (Wickham claims that Darcy failed to honor his own late father's wishes that Wickham, his godson, be provided for.) Does Elizabeth believe him? (yes) Do you?

11. What is Mr. Wickham's opinion of Mr. Darcy's sister? (that she is very proud) How does Elizabeth find out about the connection between Lady Catherine and Mr. Darcy? (When Mr. Collins mentions his patroness, Lady Catherine, Wickham mentions that Lady Catherine is Darcy's aunt, the sister of his mother.) As a reader, do you find this coincidence credible?

12. **Prediction:** Do you think Mr. Darcy will marry Miss De Bourgh?

Writing Activity
You are Mr. Darcy. Write a letter to your sister (as described on pages 41-42).

The Author's Craft: Satire
Explain that **satire** is the use of ridicule, sarcasm, wit, or irony to expose a folly or social evil. Reread the section where the narrator describes the evening conversation upon Elizabeth and Jane's return (p. 53). How is the author poking fun at the three younger sisters' values? ("Mary...deep in the study of thorough bass and human nature;" Mary takes herself—and her pessimistic view of human nature— very seriously. "Several of the officers had dined lately with their uncle, a private had been flogged, and it had actually been hinted that Colonel Forster was going to be married;" Lydia and Catherine are superficial sorts, who find the whipping of a man just one more item of entertaining news.)

Research
Find out what a "loo table" (p. 41) is.

4. According to Mr. Darcy, what are his own good and bad points? Does he think he is too proud? (He thinks he is proud when he should be, has a temper that is too rigid, doesn't forget wrongs easily, but also isn't easily manipulated.) What do you think Elizabeth would say if asked to list her strengths and faults? What are yours?

5. How does everyone feel about Jane's departure from the Bingleys', after she recuperates? (Bingley—and Jane's mother—are probably the only ones sorry to see her go.) Why is Mr. Darcy happy to see her go? (He is more interested in Elizabeth than he wants to be.) How well do you suppose he knows his own feelings?

6. Who is Mr. Collins and why does he write to Mr. Bennet? (Collins, Mr. Bennet's cousin, plans to visit.) What are your impressions of him, based on his appearance, behavior, comments, and what others say about him? (His humility is false; he seems pompous and self-righteous.)

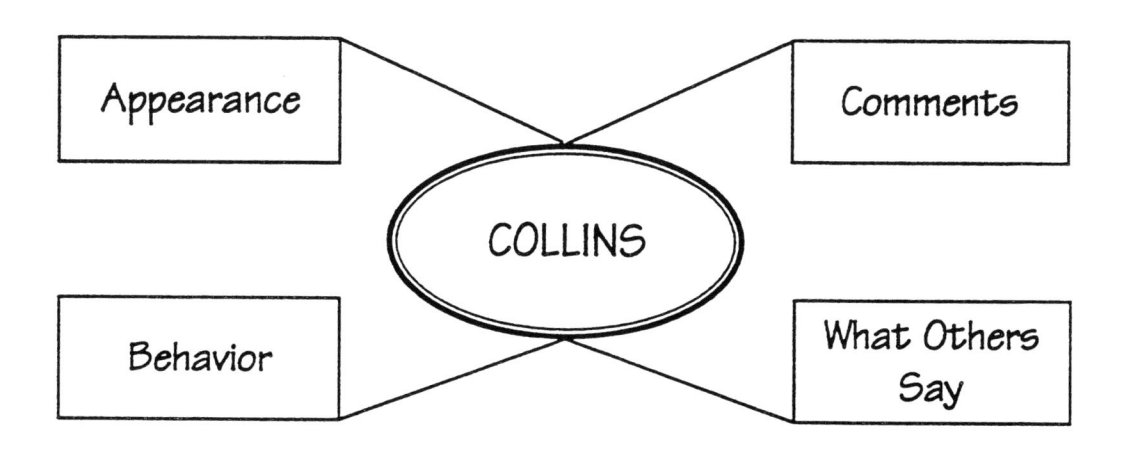

```
  Appearance                              Comments
              \      _____      /
               \    /      \    /
                 COLLINS
               /    \      /    \
              /      ‾‾‾‾‾‾      \
   Behavior                           What Others
                                          Say
```

7. Why does Mr. Collins want to offer an "olive branch"? (He wants to smooth over bad feelings about the fact that he will one day inherit Mr. Bennet's estate.) How does he plan to make amends to the Bennets? (by marrying one of their daughters) He is described as being "a mixture of pride and obsequiousness" (p. 61). Have you ever known such a person? What did he or she do that is similar to Mr. Collins' behavior?

8. Jane Austen and the rest of her family enjoyed reading novels, at a time when novel-reading was still considered suspect by many people. How is this true detail from her family life reflected in Chapter 14? (p. 59—Mr. Bennet invites Mr. Collins to read to the ladies.).

Chapters 10-17
Pages 41-77

Vocabulary

piquet 41	odious 41	disarm 42	humility 42
panegyric 43	laudable 43	celerity 43	rashness 43
obstinacy 43	deference 44	expostulation 44	alacrity 45
reprehensible 45	compass 46	affront 46	picturesque 47
studious 49	novelty 49	follies 50	pretension 50
implacable 51	propensity 51	propitious 51	uncivil 52
laconic 52	entail 54	rail 54	iniquitous 54
filial 54	beneficence 55	servility 56	destitute 57
asperity 57	affability 58	quadrille 58	parish 58
phaeton 59	importune 60	subjection 60	veneration 61
obsequiousness 61	incumbent 61	folios 62	scruples 65
digressions 65	creditable 66	whist 66	engrossing 66
inducement 68	procured 68	bequeathed 69	bequest 69
degenerate 71	amiable 71	dictatorial 73	veracity 74
alienated 74	disinclination 75	proxy 77	

Discussion Questions

1. What sort of argument arises while Mr. Darcy is writing a letter to his sister? (Mr. Darcy accuses Bingley of false humility.) What does Elizabeth mean when she asks, "In general and ordinary cases between friend and friend, where one of them is desired by the other to change a resolution of no very great moment, should you think ill of that person for complying with the desire, without waiting to be argued into it"? (p. 44) (Sometimes one friend should bend and do what the other friend wants without questioning, just to be a good friend.) Do you agree with her? Can you think of an example involving a friend and you?

2. Elizabeth notices that Mr. Darcy is watching her. What does Elizabeth make of that? (She is puzzled; thinks maybe he finds her curiously reprehensible.) What does Miss Bingley make of it? (that Darcy is interested in Elizabeth) How can you tell? (Miss Bingley acts catty and jealous.) What do you think Elizabeth would say if Jane remarked that Mr. Darcy seemed quite bewitched by Jane?

3. Why does Miss Bingley ask Elizabeth to walk around the room with her? (to get Darcy's attention) Today, what might she do to accomplish the same purpose? What do you think Miss Bingley tells herself each time Mr. Darcy ignores her or gives her a verbal put-down?

NOVEL UNITS © 1995 Anne Troy, Ph.D. and Phyllis Green, Ph.D.

16. **Prediction:** How will Mr. Darcy treat Elizabeth during their next encounter?

	Ideal Woman	
Bingley's	Darcy's	Yours

The Author's Craft: Irony
Explain that **irony** is a figure of speech in which the narrator's words really mean the opposite of what they seem to say. Point out the example on page 33.

> "...but his sisters gave it their hearty assent, and indulged their mirth for some time at the expense of their dear friend's vulgar relations."

The narrator is saying that Jane is NOT really the Bingleys' dear friend at all; they call her a friend, but in reality they laugh at her relatives behind her back. Tell students to look for other examples of irony as they read.

Writing Activities
Write a short piece of dialogue between Miss Bingley, her sister, and Mr. Darcy after Mrs. Bennet and her daughters have left. (Include Miss Bingley's "witticisms on fine eyes."—p. 41)

Write the note to Jane that either Lydia, Catherine, or Mary might send to Jane while Jane is recuperating. Keep in mind what you know so far about each of their personalities, but feel free to use your imagination to enlarge on the experiences each note might relate.

Research
Find out what Michaelmas (p. 5) is.

7. What do Mr. Darcy and Elizabeth think of each other? (Elizabeth thinks that Mr. Darcy is overly proud; he thinks that she isn't beautiful but has fine eyes.) Is each aware of the other's opinion? (no) Do these two remind you of any couples you know from TV or film?

8. What is Mary like? (She isn't very good at the piano but is vain and loves to be the center of attention.) Why do people prefer to hear Elizabeth play and sing? (She plays unaffectedly.) Do you agree with the narrator that a person who is plain may work harder to become "accomplished" (p. 23)?

9. Why does Elizabeth refuse to dance with Mr. Darcy? (She has heard him say in the past that she isn't pretty enough to get him to ask for a dance.) Is she rude? (facetious) Is he offended? (surprised)

10. What does Miss Bingley's relationship with Mr. Darcy seem to be? (She is always trying to get his attention, has her eye on him.) How does she "entertain herself" (p. 25) when she discovers that Mr. Darcy thinks that Elizabeth has "fine eyes"? (She makes snide comments about Elizabeth.)

11. Who is Mrs. Phillips? (Mrs. Bennet's sister) Why do the Bennets enjoy visiting her? (She lives in Meryton near a hatshop and near where a regiment is headquartered; she provides gossip.) Does this sound like fun to you?

12. Why does Jane send a letter to Lizzy? (She is sick with a cold at the Bingleys'.) What does each of the Bennets' reactions to the letter show about him/her? (Mr. Bennet makes a joke, Mrs. Bennet is happy that Jane will have a better opportunity to snare Mr. Bingley, Elizabeth is concerned about her sister, Mary moralizes about why Elizabeth shouldn't walk to see her and the two younger girls find in it an excuse to walk to Meryton.)

13. How does Bingley respond to Jane's illness? (concerned, wants to make her comfortable) How do his sisters respond? (seem solicitous in Jane's presence, but when she is no better, soon forget about her) Would you say that they are hypocrites? Does Elizabeth like the Bingleys? (not the sisters) Would you?

14. What is Mr. Darcy's idea of the ideal woman? (a woman who reads extensively, and has a knowledge of music, singing, drawing, dancing, and languages) What do you think Bingley's ideal is? What is yours? (use a graphic like the one on the next page to list and compare "ideals.")

15. What do Mrs. Bennet and Mr. Darcy seem to think of each other? (She finds him conceited; he finds her silly and provincial.) What do you suppose the Bingleys say about the Bennets after they are gone? Would you say that the Bingleys are catty?

NOVEL UNITS © 1995 Anne Troy, Ph.D. and Phyllis Green, Ph.D.

Discussion Questions

1. What does the statement that opens the book mean, in your own words? (Everyone knows that a single, rich man needs a wife.) In what tone do you "hear" the narrator uttering that statement? (mildly ironic) Do you agree with the statement? Why does Jane Austen begin the book with that pronouncement?

2. How do you picture Mr. and Mrs. Bennet? What sort of relationship do they have? (She complains, nags him.) Why does Mrs. Bennet want Mr. Bennet to visit Mr. Bingley? (so that Bingley will get to know them and marry one of their daughters) Why do you think Mr. Bennet does so—without telling her?

3. What do you know so far about Mr. Bingley? (rich, renting Netherfield Park, good-natured)...about Mr. Darcy? (rich, arrogant) How do you know? How are they alike? How do they differ?

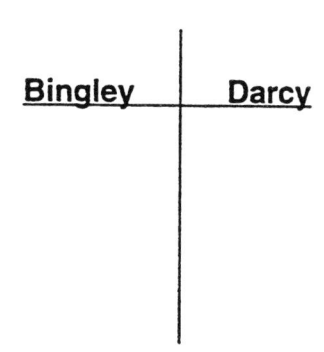

Bingley	Darcy

4. What are your impressions of the Bennet sisters? (Jane is the prettiest, Elizabeth the wittiest and most clear-sighted, Mary is pedantic and vain, Catherine and Lydia are flirts.) How would you describe their relationship with their father? (He finds them silly and amusing, but loves them. They respect him.) Which one seems closest to him? (Elizabeth)

5. Who are Charlotte and Lady Lucas? (Elizabeth's best friend and her mother) Why is Lady Lucas described as "not too clever to be a valuable neighbor to Mrs. Bennet"? (Mrs. Bennet can exploit her for gossip.) Do you agree with Charlotte that "a woman had better show more affection that she feels" (p. 20) and that "happiness in marriage is entirely a matter of chance" (p. 21)?

6. What do you think of Mr. Bingley's sisters? (conceited, catty) What do they think of the Bennets? With whom would you rather be friends?

1. Pride can get in your way when...
2. Parents want their children to marry...
3. If you're really in love...
4. When you're turned down...

12. **Debate:** Stage a classroom debate on the following:

    "Love is blind."

    Students who agree with the statement get on one side of the room and those who disagree get on the other side. Students on both sides try to convince the "undecideds" who remain in the middle.

13. **Questionnaire:** As a class, make up a list of 20 or so common statements about love and marriage. <u>Tell</u> <u>students</u>: See how other people feel about these statements by administering a survey comprised of the 20 statements (attached to a grid so that you can record agreement or disagreement). After you have questioned 10-20 people, tally the responses for each statement and discuss your results with classmates. Consider how your results apply to the novel as you read it.

Vocabulary • Discussion Questions
• • • • • • • • • • • • • Writing Ideas • Activities • • • • • • • • • • • • •

Volume 1
Chapters 1-9, Pages 5-40

Vocabulary

chaise 5	scrupulous 6	solace 7	assemblies 8
deigned 8	fortnight 8	circumspection 8	stoutly 9
disconcerted 10	countenance 11	mien 11	slighted 11
candour 15	ostentation 15	ductility 16	supercilious 17
piqued 19	impertinent 20	felicity 21	pedantic 23
complaisance 24	archly 24	reverie 24	insipidity 25
intrepidity 25	matrimony 25	milliner 26	tete-a-tete 27
extort 28	prognostics 28	benevolence 29	stiles 29
solicitude 30	apothecary 30	draughts 30	ragout 31
decorum 32	censure 33	pianoforte 34	paltry 36
civility 37	estimable 38	efficacy 40	

7. **Geography:** Before students read the story, have them locate England on a map. Ask them to find the three counties where most of the action occurs—Hertfordshire, Derbyshire, and Kent. Tell them to try to figure out which places in the story are real and which are imaginary by referring to the map as they read.

8. **Prediction:** Have students look at the cover illustration and read the title. What is **pride**? When it is it a desirable quality? When is it a bad thing? What is **prejudice**? How does it arise? To what does it lead? Based on the illustration, when would you say the story takes place? What is the relationship between the women? What can you tell about them? What examples of pride and prejudice might we meet in the novel? Will the author's treatment be serious? humorous? How will the novel make you feel? What will the story be about?

9. **Novel Sleuth:** Have students mark places where characters demonstrate self-knowledge with an **S** and places where they seem blinded by pride and/or prejudice with a **P**. Tell them that they will later use these passages in discussion and writing about themes in the novel.

10. **Pre-reading Discussion Topics**
    Love: What is your definition of love? Do you think that you can have love without physical attraction? Should two people who are in love pursue their relationship—regardless of what friends and family think? Can two people with different values be in love? How does love change after marriage? Should a husband and a wife who aren't in love—but have children—stay married? What would you say to a friend who got involved with someone—not for love, but for the material things he or she could offer?
    Parenting: What makes a good parent? How much say should a parent have in who you spend time with? What should parents do when they disagree about allowing you to do or have something?
    Siblings: What things do siblings usually have in common? Do they usually share the same values? Are they more alike in personality than any other group of people? Do siblings tend to be jealous? What would it be like to live in a family of five sisters?

11. **Pre-reading Writing:** Have students use the prompts on page 9 to freewrite (write what comes to mind without stopping to correct). You might have them choose one prompt to write a pre-reading paragraph and use the others later as starters for journal entries, or have them complete all the prompts today as single sentences.

Clear-sighted	1 2 3 4 5 6	*Foolish*
Independent	1 2 3 4 5 6	*Conforming*
Active	1 2 3 4 5 6	*Passive*
Honest	1 2 3 4 5 6	*Dishonest*
Caring	1 2 3 4 5 6	*Unkind*
Responsible	1 2 3 4 5 6	*Irresponsible*
Rich	1 2 3 4 5 6	*Poor*

5. **Brainstorming:** Have students generate associations with the phrase "pride" while a student scribe jots ideas around the central word on a large piece of paper. Help students "cluster" the ideas into categories. Repeat the process for "prejudice." A sample framework is shown below.

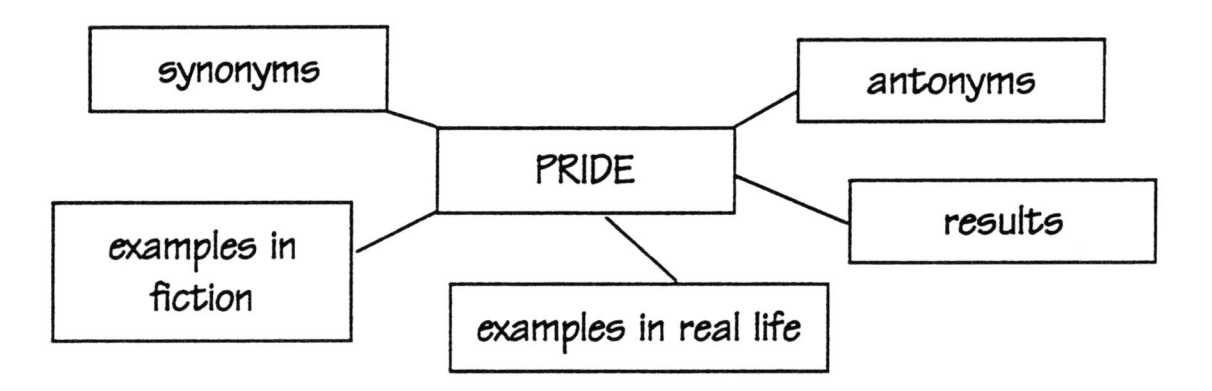

PRIDE — synonyms, antonyms, examples in fiction, examples in real life, results

6. **Role Play:** Have small groups of students improvise skits demonstrating one of the following situations (analogous to situations in the story):

- At a party, you overhear a stranger make a critical comment about you. You jokingly tell your friends about it and you all discuss your opinion of the nice-looking stranger.
- Your teenaged sister's boyfriend (or brother's girlfriend) hasn't called lately. You and your sibling discuss what this could mean and what you think he/she should do.
- You are with your family (at a party or some other event) and the way they are acting in front of your friends is really embarrassing you.

- "Love is like the measles...we all have to go through it."—Jerome Jerome, 1886
- You should never marry someone unless you love each other.
- Opposites attract.

2. **Video:** View a video version before reading the story—such as the classic with Greer Garson, Laurence Olivier and Maureen O'Sullivan (Metro/Goldwyn).

3. **Log:** Have students keep a response log as they read.

    In one type of log, the student assumes the persona of one of the characters. Using one side of each piece of paper, the student writes in the first person ("I...") about his/her reactions to that chapter. A partner (or the teacher) responds to these writings on the other side of the paper, as if talking to the character.

    In the dual entry log, students jot down brief summaries and reactions to each section of the novel they have read. (The first entry could be made based on a preview of the novel—a glance at the cover and a flip through the book.)

Pages	Summary	Reactions
		These might begin: "I liked the part where Elizabeth...," "This reminded me of the time I...," "Mrs. Bennet reminds me of another character...," "If I were Mr. Bennet, I wouldn't...," "I disagree with Jane when she says..."

    As another option, simply have students write responses to the novel on sticky notes as they read, using them for later reference during discussion.

4. **Verbal Scales:** After students finish a section of the story, have them chart their feelings/judgments about various characters using the following scales or others you construct. Students should discuss their ratings, using evidence from the story.

Like	1 2 3 4 5 6	*Dislike*
Proud	1 2 3 4 5 6	*Not Proud*
Prejudiced	1 2 3 4 5 6	*Unprejudiced*
Sensitive	1 2 3 4 5 6	*Insensitive*

NOVEL UNITS © 1995 Anne Troy, Ph.D. and Phyllis Green, Ph.D.

Background on the Novelist

Jane Austen was born in 1775 in Steventon, England, the seventh of eight children. Her father was a clergyman; both parents came from a long line of prosperous country families (headed by professionals, mainly clergymen). She led what many would consider a quiet, uneventful life, but her family was lively and intelligent—and it was that family and the neighbors around her that provided the subject matter for her work. At a time when novel-reading was still considered suspect by many, the Austens were avid novel-readers. They enjoyed amateur theatricals and provided an enthusiastic audience for the comic pieces Jane turned out as a girl. (Although she had practically no formal schooling, by age 14 Jane had written several comical parodies of contemporary literature such as Goldsmith's *History of Literature.*)

As a young adult, Jane was a prolific writer; by age 23 she had written three novels. There was a lull in her productivity between about 1800 and 1810. During that time she and her only sister, Cassandra (a lifelong intimate who, like Jane, never married) moved to Bath with their parents due to their father's failing health. After the father died in 1805, the family moved to Southampton, and moved back to the country near Jane's childhood home in 1809.

There she wrote anonymously ("by a Lady") for the last eight years of her life, turning out the six novels that have been praised for their craftsmanship and wit: *Sense and Sensibility* (1811), *Pride and Prejudice* (1813), *Mansfield Park* (1814), *Emma* (1816), *Persuasion* (1818), and *Northanger Abbey* (1818). Watched over by her family during a long illness, she was taken to Winchester for medical treatment and died there in 1817.

Initiating Activities

Choose one or more of the following activities to establish an appropriate mind set for the story students are about to read:

1. **Anticipation Guide** (See *Novel Units Student Packet,* Activity #1): Students discuss their opinions of statements which tap themes they will meet in the novel. For example:
   - You will reap what you sow. (Russian proverb: "You will be rewarded or punished according to what you have done.")
   - The tongue may speak without the head's knowing. (Foolish people often like to express their opinions.)
   - "Prejudice: a vagrant opinion without support"—Ambrose Bierce: *Devil's Dictionary,* 1911)
   - "Caution in love is perhaps the most fatal to true happiness."—Bertrand Russell

found Lydia; he has settled things and if Mr. Bennet will promise a relatively small settlement, Mr. Wickham will marry Lydia. Chapter 8: Mrs. Bennet is horrified to hear her husband refuse to spend any money on wedding clothes for Lydia; Elizabeth wishes she hadn't told Mr. Darcy about the shameful elopement. Chapter 9: Lydia's wedding day arrives; Lydia is ecstatic and mentions in describing it to her family that Mr. Darcy was present; Elizabeth writes her aunt to find out why. Chapter 10: In her response to Elizabeth, Mrs. Gardiner admits that though she has been bound to secrecy—it was Mr. Darcy who made a financial settlement with Wickham and it is to Darcy that the Bennets owe the salvation of their family's name. Chapter 11: Lydia and Mr. Wickham depart, and after an absence of many months, Mr. Bingley pays a call along with his friend, Mr. Darcy; Elizabeth is pleased to see that Mr. Bingley's admiration of Jane is rekindled. Chapter 12: As Mr. Darcy plays whist at another table, Elizabeth finds herself scarcely daring to wish that he who has been refused might renew his love. Chapter 13: Bingley declares his love for Jane and becomes a daily visitor at Longbourn. Chapter 14: A week after Jane's engagement, the Bennets are surprised to have Lady Catherine de Bourgh pay a call. Lady Catherine tells Elizabeth that she has heard reports—which she insists Elizabeth deny—that Elizabeth and Mr. Darcy will soon be wed. Elizabeth admits there is no engagement, but refuses to promise never to enter into one, and Lady Catherine leaves in a huff. Chapter 15: Elizabeth worries how Mr. Darcy will react when his aunt points out to him his duty not to marry someone who is "beneath" him; Mr. Collins writes to Mr. Bennet, warning against Elizabeth's accepting Mr. Darcy's proposals; unsuspecting Mr. Bennet laughs at the absurdity of the idea of such a match. Chapter 16: Mr. Bingley and Mr. Darcy arrive at Longbourn; Elizabeth takes Mr. Darcy aside and thanks him for helping her sister; Mr. Darcy has spoken with his aunt—and is more in love than ever with Elizabeth; he acknowledges that while he once kept Bingley ignorant of the fact that Jane was in London, he has since assured his friend that the match meets with his approval. Chapter 17: Mr. Darcy asks Mr. Bennet for Elizabeth's hand; she manages to convince her father that she does indeed love the man she formerly reproached. Mrs. Bennet is beside herself with happiness when she hears of the engagement between her "Lizzy" and wealthy Mr. Darcy, and quickly dismisses her prejudice against him. Chapter 18: Elizabeth writes to Mrs. Gardiner of her happy engagement; Mr. Darcy writes a letter that infuriates his aunt, announcing the engagement; Mr. Bennet writes a snide note to Mr. Collins with the news. ("Console Lady Catherine as well as you can. But, if I were you, I would stand by the nephew. He has more to give.") Chapter 19: To Mrs. Bennet's joy, Jane and Elizabeth are married; Mr. Bingley and Jane move to an estate in a neighboring county. Catherine profits from spending most of her time with her two older sisters; Lydia and Wickham continue to spend more money than they have and move from place to place; Mary stays at home with her mother; Mr. Darcy's aunt condescends to visit the couple in Pemberley; Darcy and Elizabeth enjoy the visits of the Gardiners, who brought them together that fateful day while on their tour of Derbyshire.

NOVEL UNITS © 1995 Anne Troy, Ph.D. and Phyllis Green, Ph.D.

detect any sign of affection between Mr. Darcy and his purportedly intended, the sickly Miss De Bourgh. Chapter 9: Mr. Darcy comes often to the parsonage and Charlotte suggests that he may be partial to Elizabeth, who scoffs at the idea. Chapter 10: Col. Fitzwilliam tells Elizabeth that Bingley is indebted to Mr. Darcy for saving him from an imprudent marriage; Elizabeth is outraged to find out Mr. Darcy's role in her sister's unhappiness. Chapter 11: To Elizabeth's astonishment, Mr. Darcy requests her hand in marriage, while pointing out the obstacles posed by her family's inferiority. Elizabeth angrily rejects him, emphasizing her disdain for someone who could wrong both Jane and Wickham as he has. Chapter 12: Elizabeth receives a letter from Mr. Darcy in which he explains his side of things; he sincerely did not believe that Jane felt a serious attachment to Bingley. As for Wickham, the scoundrel squandered his legacy, asked for more money to study law rather than take the proffered "living" in the clergy; squandered that and demanded the clergy position after all; when Mr. Darcy refused, Wickham ran off with Mr. Darcy's young sister, but Darcy was able to rescue her and prevent gossip. Chapter 13: Elizabeth is ashamed to think that she had been so blind to the truth about Wickham. Chapter 14: Elizabeth prepares to return home to her family; upon reading and rereading the letter, she decides that she respects Mr. Darcy, but does not want to see him again. Chapter 15: Elizabeth, Sir William and Maria stay with the Gardiners for a few days. Chapter 16: Elizabeth is welcomed home; her sisters mention that the officers are leaving soon for Brighton, where the girls are trying unsuccessfully to convince Mr. Bennet to take the family for the summer. Chapter 17: Elizabeth tells Jane of rejecting Mr. Darcy's proposal and of Wickham's true nature, but does not mention his role in separating Jane from Mr. Bingley. Chapter 18: Lydia is invited to Brighton by the wife of the regiment's colonel. Chapter 19: Elizabeth goes on a trip with the Gardiners, and agrees to stop at Pemberley to see Mr. Darcy's estate, once she is reassured that the owner will not be there.

Volume 3
Chapter 1: Elizabeth is mortified when Mr. Darcy shows up earlier than expected at his estate and finds her there; she is surprised by his civility toward her and her relations and astounded by his request that she meet his sister. Chapter 2: Elizabeth finds that Mr. Darcy's sister is shy, not overly proud as had been reported by Wickham; Mr. and Mrs. Gardiner suspect that Mr. Darcy is in love with their niece; Bingley comes for a visit and Elizabeth senses he would like to talk about Jane. Chapter 3: Miss Bingley, who still has designs on Mr. Darcy, is not pleased to find Elizabeth at Pemberley. Chapter 4: Jane writes with the distressing news that Lydia has run off with Wickham; Elizabeth bursts into tears as she tells Mr. Darcy what has happened. Chapter 5: Elizabeth returns home and Mr. Gardiner agrees to help Mr. Bennet recover Lydia; Elizabeth blames herself for not revealing earlier what she knew about Wickham's true disposition. Chapter 6: Mr. Collins writes a letter of condolence to the Bennets; Mr. Bennet returns from London empty-handed. Chapter 7: Mr. Gardiner writes that he has

who will inherit Mr. Bennet's estate, as per Mr. Bennet's father's will ("entailing" the estate so that his children—all female—will not inherit). Chapter 14: Mr. Collins is lavish in his praise of his patroness, Lady Catherine de Bourgh. Chapter 15: Mr. Collins has come to find a wife and Mrs. Bennet indicates that Elizabeth is available. Elizabeth notices that Mr. Darcy has given the cold shoulder to Mr. Wickham, a handsome new officer who has caught the ladies' attention. Chapter 16: Wickham tells Elizabeth that he has been ill-used by Mr. Darcy, who ignored his late father's bequest of a living to Wickham, the son of the elder Darcy's steward. Wickham reveals that Lady Catherine de Bourgh is Mr. Darcy's aunt, and that Lady Catherine's daughter is expected to marry Mr. Darcy, uniting the two estates. Chapter 17: The Bennets are invited to the Bingleys' ball at Netherfield, and Elizabeth looks forward to dancing with Wickham. Chapter 18: When Wickham doesn't show up at the dance, his friend Denny reveals that he is avoiding Mr. Darcy. Mr. Collins monopolizes most of Elizabeth's time, but she does dance with Mr. Darcy. Miss Bingley tells Elizabeth that it is Mr. Wickham who has mistreated Mr. Darcy, and Mr. Bingley tells Jane that Wickham is not a respectable man. Elizabeth is mortified by her family's embarrassing behavior at the dance. Chapter 19: Mr. Collins proposes to Elizabeth and she refuses. Chapter 20: Mrs. Bennet insists that Jane accept the proposal, to no avail. Chapter 21: Jane is upset by a letter from Miss Bingley which reveals that the Bingleys have left Netherfield for London and do not intend to return. Elizabeth suspects that Bingley's sisters are trying to prevent a match between their brother and Jane. Chapter 22: Elizabeth is shocked to find that Mr. Collins has asked her friend Charlotte to marry him—and she has accepted! Chapter 23: Mr. Collins stays with the Bennets while courting Charlotte. Mrs. Bennet is inconsolable.

Volume 2
Chapter 1: Jane is miserable, but cannot bring herself to blame Mr. Bingley's sisters for wanting him to choose Miss Darcy over herself. Chapter 2: The Gardiners, Mrs. Bennet's brother and his wife, come to spend Christmas at Longbourn. Elizabeth, who is close to her aunt, confides in her about Jane's broken love affair. Mrs. Gardiner promptly invites Jane to London. Chapter 3: Mrs. Gardiner warns Elizabeth against getting involved with Wickham, who has no money. Charlotte and Mr. Collins are married; Jane writes that she has visited Miss Bingley in London, but that she has not been warmly received. Elizabeth writes to her aunt that Wickham has turned his attentions to a Miss King, who has recently come into an inheritance. Chapter 4: Elizabeth goes with Sir William Lucas and his daughter to Hunsford to visit Charlotte. Chapter 5: Lady Catherine honors Mr. Collins with her presence and invites the party to dine at her estate, Rosings. Chapter 6: In conversation with arrogant Lady Catherine, Elizabeth astonishes her hostess by daring to stand up for herself and her family. Chapter 7: Mr. Darcy arrives with Col. Fitzwilliam, the younger son of his uncle. Chapter 8: At Col. Fitzwilliam's request, Elizabeth plays the pianoforte; she cannot

Plot Summary

Pride and Prejudice is Jane Austen's witty masterpiece about husband-hunting in the comfortable English country society in which she lived. The story takes place at the turn of the 18th century, but the themes still have appeal for today's students—a Cinderella love story, growth in self-knowledge, back-stabbing among "friends," interference by parents, marital tensions, sibling strife. Austen has a mercilessly acute sense of social satire, and students today will still recognize many of the elements at which she pokes fun—class consciousness, materialism, snobbery, the difficulty men and women often have in expressing themselves directly.

Volume 1
Chapter 1: The story opens with Mrs. Bennet's announcement to her husband that a rich, eligible bachelor is about to take up residence at nearby Netherfield Park. Mrs. Bennet urges her husband to visit their new neighbor soon—for their five daughters' sake. Chapter 2: Mr. Bennet teasingly reveals to his happy brood that he has paid a call on Mr. Bingley. Chapter 3: Mr. Bingley returns the visit, and a few days later arrives at a local ball with his small party (comprised of his two sisters, a brother-in-law, and a friend, Mr. Darcy). Mr. Bingley dances happily with Jane, the oldest and prettiest sister in the Bennet family; Elizabeth, on the other hand, is slighted by Bingley's haughty friend, Mr. Darcy. Elizabeth enjoys playfully spreading the story of how she overheard Mr. Darcy declare that she was not handsome enough to tempt him to dance with her. Chapter 4: After the ball, Jane praises Mr. Bingley to Elizabeth, and Mr. Bingley praises Jane to Mr. Darcy. Chapter 5: Lady Lucas and her daughter Charlotte pay a call to discuss the ball with the Bennets; Charlotte feels that Mr. Darcy has a right to be proud, but her friend Elizabeth points out that he mortified her own pride. Chapter 6: Mr. Darcy asks Elizabeth to dance and she refuses, unaware that he has begun to take an interest in her. Chapter 7: Caroline Bingley invites Jane over; while at Netherfield, Jane comes down with a cold and is put to bed. Lydia and Catherine go off to flirt with some officers while Elizabeth walks to Netherfield to be with Jane. Chapter 8: The Bingley sisters criticize Elizabeth behind her back. Mr. Darcy spars with Elizabeth about what constitutes an "accomplished" woman and Mr. Bingley busies himself in making Jane comfortable. Chapter 9: Mrs. Bennet and her daughters visit Netherfield Park; Mrs. Bennet declares that Jane is too ill to be moved and returns home. Chapter 10: Mr. Darcy writes a letter to his sister while Miss Bingley tries unsuccessfully to flirt with him. Mr. Darcy's interest in Elizabeth becomes increasingly evident to a jealous and increasingly catty Miss Bingley. Chapter 11: Elizabeth tells Mr. Darcy that his defect is a propensity to hate everybody. Chapter 12: To Mrs. Bennet's dismay, Jane and Elizabeth borrow a carriage and return home; Mr. Darcy resolves to be careful not to show that he admires Elizabeth. Chapter 13: Mr. Bennet's cousin, pompous Mr. Collins, writes that he is coming for a visit. The Bennets waste no affection on this clergyman,

NOVEL UNITS © 1995 Anne Troy, Ph.D. and Phyllis Green, Ph.D.

Table of Contents

Plot Summary 1

Background on the Novelist 5

Initiating Activities 5

Anticipation Guide, Viewing, Log, Verbal Scales,
Brainstorming, Role Play, Geography, Prediction,
Novel Sleuth, Discussion Topics,
Writing, Debate, Questionnaire

**Vocabulary, Discussion Questions,
Writing Ideas, Activities**

Volume One
Chapters 1-9 9
Chapters 10-17 13
Chapters 18-23 16

Volume Two
Chapters 1-10 18
Chapters 11-19 21

Volume Three
Chapters 1-5 23
Chapters 6-11 25
Chapters 12-19 28

Post-Reading Extension Activities 23

Discussion Questions, Further Reading and
Viewing, Writing, Listening/Speaking, Drama,
Dance, Language Study, Art, Music, Research,
Current Events

Pride and Prejudice

by
Jane Austen

Teacher Guide
Written by:
Gloria Levine, M.A.
Mary L. Dennis, Editor

Note
The text used to prepare this guide was the Signet Classic softcover with an afterword by Joann Morse. If other editions are used, page references may vary slightly.

ISBN 1-56137-766-X

Novel Units

P.O. Box 1461
Palatine, IL 60078

Telephone (800) 424-2084

© 1995 Novel Units. All rights reserved. Printed in the United States of America.

Limited reproduction permission: The publisher grants permission to individual teachers who have purchased this book, or for whom it has been purchased, to reproduce the blackline masters as needed for use with their own students. Reproduction for an entire school or school district or for commercial use is prohibited.